ROUGH START

SCREAMING DEMONS MC
BOOK ONE

SUMMER COOPER
SIENNA CHANCE

LOVY BOOKS

Tap, tap, tap.

Eliana drummed her finger pensively on the side of her amber coffee mug as she stared vacantly at the newspaper that lay open on her round dining table. Her chestnut-colored eyes were glazed over, a sure sign her thoughts were far away. The sun had only just crested the horizon, and from the east-facing window of her suburban home in Concord, the light was casting an orange haze throughout the kitchen. Light refracted off the glistening ink of the newspaper. Eliana took a step forward from her position leaning against the counter to lessen the glare from the image she'd been transfixed on.

There it was again. In all its dreadful glory, staring up at her in an almost taunting manner, was the nearly page-sized portrait of her father. Right at the top of the obituary section. It must have been the extra money she spent for the space that made his notoriety so prominent, Lord knows it wasn't on the merit of his conduct that gave him the honored position at the top of the page.

Henry Granville, born April 2nd, 1958, passed peacefully in sleep on the 10th of September 2019.

Born and raised in rural Maine, Henry worked with dedication for over three decades at Pine Hill Lumber Mill. His late wife passed only six years after their marriage, leaving him a single father to their daughter, and his only surviving family, Eliana. He was a loving father, loyal, hardworking…

Blah. Blah. Blah.

Setting her cup down with force onto the table, Eliana paced to the window and stared angrily at the front lawn. Her hands gripped the windowsill, knuckles white with strain. Her breathing had become more ragged, and the heat in her chest was rising to the back of her neck. Why the words made her so angry was nearly comical. Hadn't she written them herself? As a young but accomplished defense attorney, she wasn't one for fiction writing. Maybe this was one last attempt to be a good daughter. A short story of wishful thinking that would make her father—her dead father—proud.

Memories of their last encounter together flooded her mind. Pale. Sickly ill and though largely obese, he'd seemed too frail in the hospital bed with tubes in every orifice, monitors beeping and humming. His murky eyes had been searching the room frantically, his hands gripped the sheets in terror as he struggled for his next breath. The lung cancer had won. Eliana had been caught by his right hand. With strange force, he'd pulled her close, nearly toppling her on the bed, and he'd pressed his thumb firmly into her palm. Eliana stared in horror as he sputtered his last breath.

Despite her perfectly working lungs, Eliana felt herself clutching at her throat as though suffocating as she forced the memory out of her mind. Her left hand still hurt where he'd driven his thumb into her palm. Her anger as her own lies in the obituary faded into a strange feeling somewhere between grief and pity. How terrible it would be to suffocate to death. Betrayed by your own body.

Cancer is a bitch, she thought scornfully.

Startled by the hiss of the coffee maker, she turned from the window and switched the machine off. Her eyes caught the time, and she cursed under her breath. She was going to be late. Darting from the kitchen and down the hall, she raced up the stairs and into the bathroom that adjoined her yellow and teal decorated bedroom.

As she opened the door, vapor poured out like fog, and Eliana turned the shower off. Using the shower to steam clean her black dress, she pulled it free from the hanger on the shower rod and stepped into her room. Her bathrobe fell in a pool around her feet before she stepped into the tea length, cotton-blend dress that was trimmed with lace.

She was still struggling to slip her heels on as she descended the stairs and into the kitchen. With one arm in her khaki pea-coat, she pulled a tumbler from the cupboard and set it next to her forgotten mug. With haste, she poured the contents of the coffee pot into the traveler, nearly half sloshing onto the table, before she screwed the lid on, grabbed her purse and car keys from the entryway, and left the house, locking the door behind her.

Unable to help it, she found herself staring back at her home of only fourteen months in the rearview mirror of her silver Mercedes. The perfectly situated white house was in the exact center of the cul-de-sac. She'd fallen in love with it the moment the realtor had suggested it. It was the first house she'd been able to buy, and it stood as a mark of pride. How far she'd come in the last three years since she'd graduated from Harvard. Even farther in the last ten when she'd moved from Maine.

How different it was from the house she'd grown up in. The town. The people… how different she was now.

* * *

THIRTY-EIGHT. There were thirty-eight people at the funeral. Eliana knew this because, from her standing position in the back of the church, she had counted them over and over again. The hour drive from her home to the steeple-capped building hadn't been long enough. Sixty minutes wasn't enough time to prepare herself for the blur of the funeral.

Among the thirty-eight people, she'd counted twelve cousins, two aunts, six uncles; a few of her father's former co-workers and at least a dozen others who'd probably only wandered in for the food. She could feel the bitter scowl on her face, but she was startled as every single face turned from the front of the church to look at her. All thirty-eight of them. Standing more erect, her eyes darted to the minister who was looking at her expectantly.

"Miss Granville?" the middle-aged, yellow-haired minister-for-hire asked, "You… had a few words?"

"Oh!" was all she could say as she pushed herself forward. Her heels clicked on the wood floor as she walked up the aisle, and shook the reverend's hand before taking her place behind the pulpit, the open casket at her back.

We've gathered here today… she thought sardonically as she fished into the pocket of her dress and removed her notecards.

"Um…" she muttered as she straightened her immaculately constructed eulogy. "My father… Henry… Um…" For some reason, her cards were impossible to read. Why were they blurry? Looking up momentarily she realized the entire church and its thirty-eight onlookers were blurry as well. Touching a hand to her face she realized the culprit of her sudden case of vision loss wasn't cataracts, but tears. She was crying. "I'm sorry I'm…" Her heart began racing, and she feared she was about to lose all composure. Public speaking was never a paralyzing fear for her, but public blubbering was another matter altogether.

Wiping her eyes with the back of her hand, she forced a small laugh to attempt to ease the tensions within herself.

"My father was a hardworking man who had no time for sentiment," she began, eyes still stinging painfully, "or tears." A few among them chuckled. God bless her sensible cousins. "Let's be honest, we all knew a different side of Henry Granville. At work, he was devoted, clever, and painfully faithful. His crew were like brothers to him. More-so than his actual brothers." A few more laughs gave her encouragement. "Among his family, he was the life of the party. I think he laughed more at the reunions than anyone. Especially after a few drinks… he was a man who enjoyed a good drink. Or a bad one, he wasn't picky. You weren't any help with that peach moonshine you peddled that weekend at Moosehead Lake, Uncle Ron!" The assembly roared with laughter, including the red-faced man in the second row. "At home, my dad was…" She felt a sudden lump in her throat. "My dad… he…"

The stinging in her eyes had returned, and instinctively she turned her back to the room forgetting that in that motion she came face to face with the lifeless body of her father who rested in the casket. A sudden wave of nausea hit her, and her already tear-dampened hands were useless as she tried to quell the onslaught of tears.

Staring bluntly and boldly at her clearly deceased father, she couldn't help but come to the realization that her tears were not entirely of loss, but, God help her, they were in relief. He was gone, and with him the dread she'd lived with every day. She'd never again come home to find him passed out drunk on the floor having pissed himself in the process. There would never be another missed event, argument, drunken rage or emotional breakdown. Eliana would never have to endure another broken promise or failed attempt at sobriety or disappointment from him again.

He was gone. Forever.

With one hand over her mouth, she silenced the maddening laughter that threatened to burst forth.

From behind her, she could hear the murmuring and whispering that was steadily growing louder. Among the voices, a single bold and heavy footfall rattled the ground, and Eliana felt a figure approach. Thank heaven the minister was coming to relieve her failed speech.

A strong hand held a tissue to her, and she turned just enough to accept it. However, the figure next to her was far too tall to be Reverend Matthew. "Thank you…"

Drying her eyes, she looked from the ground where her cream-colored heels were pointed toward a set of large, black leather boots, up dark denim jeans covering broad thighs and hips. A black leather cut was draped over a crisp white button-down shirt that was left open at the collar revealing tanned skin at the throat and did nothing to conceal the hardened chest beneath. Dark stubble dusted a pointed chin, square jaw, and faded into slicked back black hair that curled ever so slightly at the ends. Light blue eyes grew darker toward the pupils that stared down at her.

"Kye?"

ELIANA WAS SHAMELESSLY SEARCHING for him. He could tell by the way her eyes danced around the room even while engaged in conversation with others. Despite his height, he prided himself on his ability to fade into the background and go unnoticed. It was easier to stay distant. Kye Driscoll had learned at an early age to be observant at all costs. Observant and distant.

He'd meant to keep his presence at the funeral secret, but when he'd watched Eliana struggling he was unable to keep himself tucked away. Her relatives among the pews hadn't the sense to come to her aid so he'd stepped up to the task.

Eliana was never a woman to seem meek. Perhaps that was why it pained him to watch her struggling to contain her emotions. Despite her taller than average height, especially in those shoes that made her slender legs look a mile long, she'd seemed so childlike and small. Seeing her again was like stepping back in time. Her hair was shorter now than he remembered. Probably opting for a more modern cut, the chocolate tresses she'd since straightened were cut into a smart bob, the length of which barely brushed the tops of her shoulders. With her back turned he'd been granted a view of the milky skin of her neck. She'd finally looked up at him through tear-soaked eyelashes, and he'd almost reached a hand up to take her by the neck and keep her face fixed toward his.

Almost.

Now as he watched her dance between attendants who were happy enough to keep themselves fed, he quietly followed her from the church as she made her way to the front parking lot. She stood with her back to him, giving him another glorious view of the soft skin of the back of her neck, arms wrapped around herself at the impending cold of autumn. Head turning from side to side, she spotted his motorcycle parked on the grass under the overhanging beech tree.

She moved quickly toward the v-twin engine Shadow that stood out amongst the four-door cars and vans on the gravel lot. Kye finally relented to put her out of her misery as she clearly wasn't going to stop searching until she found him. The sheen of midnight blue paint reflected her face as he stood behind her. Seeing his own face looking at her, she turned around quickly to look up at him once again, only this time her eyes were wide and dry.

"I-I was looking for you," she admitted, her left hand resting on one of the handlebars. It didn't escape his notice that her hand remained ring-less.

"You found me," he replied shortly.

"Rather you found me," she stated, having regained herself from surprise. "I couldn't believe it was you. I've felt surrounded by ghosts today."

"The past has a way of feeling like that," Kye said and lifted his right hand, the one that brandished a rather prominent silver ring with the letters SD, to brush the hair off her shoulder. She shivered.

"Kye…" she spoke his name, and he felt the hair on

his arms prickle. "Thank you for earlier. I was making a spectacle of myself up there."

"Some things never change," he cooed with a grin. "You were never one for subtlety."

"One of us had to be blunt," Eliana defended, her light brown eyes full of defiance. Their eyes locked, and the air between them felt charged as though humming with electricity. Behind them, the church bells began to toll, and Kye used her momentary distraction as the crowd began to pour out of the stone structure, to take her wrist firmly and pull her to the opposite side of the tree out of sight. "Kye!" she cried as he pressed her back against the trunk, and his hand flew to her mouth to silence her.

His breathing was coming in short rasps, and with one hand over her mouth, the other on the tree above her head, there was barely a whisper of air between them. Indeed, when she took a sharp breath her chest brushed his, and Kye squeezed his eyes shut. They remained like that for several long moments until the rumble of vehicles departing had ceased. He could sense her discomfort as she began to squirm, and he pressed his hand more firmly against her lips.

"Eli, listen to me," he demanded, his voice eerily deep and calm. When he opened his eyes again to look down at her, it wasn't with familiarity or friendliness; not even with attraction and lust, but with a warning. She stilled instantly. "I came here for a reason. There has been a long-standing debt between your father and the Screaming Demons. One that I'm sent to collect on." Her eyes went from wide and fearful to narrowed and angry in an instant. She pulled his hand off her mouth and gave his chest a firm shove.

"My father's dealings with your gang don't include me. I've paid enough of a price for his involvement." She made to walk away, but Kye took her by the waist and had her up against the tree again in a flash.

"You might think you've paid, but the debt Henry accrued is much higher than your meager pains…"

"Meager?" She spat, pushing against him again. "Meager? You really are a bastard, aren't you?"

"Yes. I am."

"Then what, money is it? How much did he take?"

"Fifty thousand."

"Fifty thousand?"

"Plus ten years interest. Likely more for the insult of betrayal."

"That could be any amount. Hundreds of thousands. A million? They don't pay twenty-eight-year-old lawyers that much, Kye. Might as well have saved yourself the trip."

"A life." His short sentence had her balking. "A life," he repeated. "Yours. I've come to collect. Today."

2

―――――――

PAST

*S*now crunched underfoot. The weeks of snow were recently dusted with fresh powder, and as Eliana walked, hands tucked in the pockets of her thick coat, she smiled as she approached the playground on the corner of the block. It was late. The moon was high overhead and shone like a polished mirror behind the white clouds. It was a quiet evening, her footfalls the only sound until she saw him sitting on the swing staring at something in his lap. Quietly setting her book bag down, she picked up a pile of snow and pressed it together between her mittens.

Kye toppled backward in alarm as something struck

the top of his head. For a moment, he thought the sky had fallen, but the ringing laughter from his friend told him otherwise. Sitting up in the snow, he hurled a snowball back at her, and Eliana cowered away from the icy onslaught.

"So not only are you late, but you assault me? Friend of the year award, right here!" Kye called sarcastically as he stood to his feet and brushed the snow off of him.

"You'll be eating those words when you see what I've brought you," Eliana replied as she fell in step with him, and they began walking toward the far end of the playground where a frozen pond was nearly concealed by the ivy branches of a towering willow tree.

"Presents?" Kye asked with a boyish lilt. Eliana giggled and ducked under the tree where the silvery, icy tendrils blocked out the rest of the world. They'd spent a week that summer building a rope ladder that led upward to a platform nailed between two dense branches. Eliana climbed first and was rummaging in her backpack by the time Kye reached the top.

"Here," she said, handing over a white paper sack with red letters.

"Mmm God, you're a Saint," he said, digging into the food sack and sinking his teeth into a still piping hot burger.

"Please don't call me that," Eliana said quietly. Kye

looked over at her, replaying his sentence, and grimaced.

"Sorry, Eli, I forgot," he apologized. Eliana flashed him a forgiving smile and pulled out two cups of hot chocolate. Passing one over, she scowled as Kye took it.

"Where are your gloves?" she practically shrieked. Kye shrugged, his mouth still full of food, and he made to pull his hand away when Eliana grabbed it and held his hand firmly between both of hers. "They're like ice cubes." He was all too familiar with her tone of voice. She was scolding him. Her raised eyebrows hinted at her demand for an explanation.

"Liam needed a pair, so I gave him mine. It's no big deal. I'm hot-blooded," he excused. Eliana's look turned to compassion, and she scooted over to sit next to him, their backs pressed against the trunk of the tree and their legs extended in front of them.

"You're a good brother," she said, still holding his left hand between hers. She'd subconsciously began rubbing them together for warmth. "You should have said something to the Duncans."

"I heard them talking last night," Kye said, swallowing his mouthful. "Liam is getting transferred to a foster center in Oregon. There's a couple there who want to adopt him…"

"Oh, Kye…"

"He'll like it better there. It's warmer. Plus, he'll have

a home soon…" Kye began picking at his thumbnail. It was a nervous habit he had. Eliana placed both of her hands over his to stop him.

"You'll make yourself bleed," she cautioned with an almost motherly tone.

"I'm so tired of saying goodbye," he admitted. "I get it, I'm almost eighteen. I have a better chance of winning a gold medal in women's gymnastics than getting adopted, but just once can't anyone… I don't know… not leave?"

"Liam will miss you; you've been a great big brother."

"But I'm not his brother!" Kye snapped, and Eliana clamped her mouth shut. They sat for several long moments in silence, his hand still grasped between her mitten clad hands. "Sorry…" he muttered.

"Don't be," Eliana said, gripping his hand tighter. "Maybe he'll come visit."

"Yeah, maybe," Kye agreed with a small smile, although they both knew the untruth of it. Kye had watched several younger siblings come and go during his time in foster care. Already on his sixth home in three years, he'd nearly mastered the art of saying good-bye. "I start my job at Hal's Garage tomorrow."

"That's great!" Eliana proclaimed, internally grateful for the subject change. "Beats working at Speedy's Eats," she teased as she took hold of the fast-food bag and began munching on the leftover French fries.

"It had its perks, I'm sure," Kye said, digging into the bag.

"Only thing I liked about that job was quitting at the end of the summer," she argued.

"It was fun coming to visit you, though."

"You liked the free food."

"Most definitely," he agreed, and they both laughed.

"Well you try washing the smell of grease out of your hair," she challenged. Dragging her long ponytail over her shoulder, she ran her hands over the straight tresses.

"I imagine that would take you a while with all that hair," Kye teased, and she nudged his shoulder with her own. He couldn't help his smile as he watched her playing with her hair. Had it not been for the nearly waist-length strands, they may have never met.

At the beginning of the summer, they'd both been in the same SAT prep course before they'd taken their college placements. Feeling years behind due to moving up and down the East Coast, hopping from foster home to foster home, Kye's new guardians, Carey and Stan Duncan, had enrolled him. Kye had already been seated when the tall brunette entered the room and sat at the desk in front of him. The moment he saw her he sat a little straighter.

An hour into their first practice test she'd flipped her hair over her shoulder and had practically covered half his paper. Chuckling to himself, he prodded her shoulder with his pencil, and she'd laughed sheepishly and muttered a soft apology. Eliana bound her hair into a high ponytail, liberating his exam and nearly his senses. The scent of citrus from her shampoo and the nine freckles on the back of her neck were far more distracting.

"What are you thinking about?" Eliana asked as she noticed his vacant stare.

"Your hair," he chided, and she rolled her eyes.

"I'm going to cut it all off," she declared.

"Don't you dare," Kye warned, and they met eyes. "Your hair is beautiful. Even if it does smell like burger grease."

"Bully! I'm never bringing you food again!" Eliana shrieked, and Kye burst into laughter. She gave him a firm shove for good measure, and he responded by wrapping her in a bear hug, arms pinned to her sides. "Kye!"

"Take it back!" he goaded as she struggled to break free.

"Never!"

"Take it back, Eli. I'm not letting you go until you do!" Squirming with all her might, Eliana only managed to fall onto her side, Kye's full weight pressing her into the platform.

"Damn you and your one season of wrestling," she cursed and went limp. "Fine, I take it back. I'll bring you all the food." Kye's body was shaking from laughter, and he shifted his torso, to her surprise, so he was laying over her propped up on his forearms. "Kye…" she breathed as he looked down at her. His eyes still glinting with mischief, but his face growing more serious.

"Eli?" he asked, both suddenly speaking in softer tones.

"Hmm?" she responded, feeling it was harder to breathe with him looking at her like that as opposed to when he had her in a bear lock. His icy, ungloved hand lifted to brush her cheek as he tucked a lock of hair behind her ear, his touch giving her a wave of chills.

"Don't cut your hair," he requested, and she felt a small smile pull at her mouth.

"Okay," she agreed. Eliana knew the second his eyes moved from her eyes to her lips, and she felt blood rush to her head and her breathing stop altogether. His hands didn't move, but his face was definitely getting closer. "Kye, are you…" …going to kiss me? That had been what she'd wanted to ask. What she'd meant to ask. Like the rush of winter wind that had blown the snowstorm through, she'd suddenly, and frustratingly, remembered the whole reason she had text him asking him to meet her.

She was leaving.

Kye felt the moment her body went rigid. Her sharp intake of breath might as well have been a second shove.

He flew off her so fast he nearly toppled over the end of the platform and the twenty feet to the ground. Eliana sat upright and pulled her knit cap more securely onto her head. She didn't know whether to apologize or burst into tears. Had her logical brain just ruined her only chance to have a first kiss with Kye?

"I didn't mean…" she began to apologize.

"No, I'm sorry. I didn't mean to…"

"I wasn't telling you to stop…"

"I made you uncomfortable…"

"No, really, you didn't…"

"It won't happen again."

"It won't?" Her question was so quiet he barely heard it. Meeting her eyes again, he had to smirk at her rounded eyes and blushing cheeks. Their summer together as fast friends had slowly been turning into something else, and for weeks now he'd been wanting to kiss her. There always seemed to be something holding him back. Maybe it was his expertise in saying goodbye. He knew eventually Eliana would be just another farewell. Just the thought of that made his throat constrict.

"We killed the food," he noted as he held up the squashed bag. Eliana couldn't help but laugh, and Kye joined in.

"At least the hot cocoa survived," she said, passing him the cup. Kye took a long drink before handing the lukewarm beverage back to her. A long moment of quiet passed between them. The tension of awkwardness was still wafting in the air, but the two settled back against the trunk of the tree, huddled close for warmth, and the serenity of their friendship took over.

"I was going to tell you," Eliana began as she stared at the toes of her boots. "I heard back from the administrative office from Harvard today."

"You did?" Kye's excitement matched her own, though she felt she needed to keep it concealed for the moment. "Did they send you an acceptance letter?"

"Something like that," she muttered. In truth, she'd not only received an acceptance letter, but also a phone call. The phone call. Four years' worth of spring breaks Eliana had dedicated herself to building houses with Habitat for Humanity in the Boston area. Not just out of humanitarianism, but strategy. The Wendell Hall scholarship was her prize. It required over five hundred hours of community service, a written recommendation from a local politician, a GPA of no less than 4.0 and a ten-page letter explaining her qualifications, but she'd done it. Eliana was awarded one of only four scholarships a year that ensured her place among the Ivy League.

So, why did she feel sad?

"Eli tha-that's amazing! You're going to Harvard!" Kye flew to his feet. "Hey, everyone!" he beckoned to the empty park. "My friend Eliana Granville is going to Harvard University!"

"Kye!" Eliana cried as she tugged on his hand. Her admonishment fell on deaf ears as, instead of pulling him down, he yanked her to her feet.

"Did you hear me? Harvard University!"

"No, I'm not!" she yelled over him, and he quieted. She was holding on to him for balance, and Kye was slightly ducked to miss hitting his head on the branches above them.

"What do you mean you're not?"

"I mean … I don't know yet."

"Didn't they accept you?" he asked with a furrowed brow.

"They did, it's just … um… I don't think I can afford to go."

"What about that scholarship thing? Isn't it a full ride?"

"I-I haven't heard back yet, so I can't get too excited. Yet." Shifting her weight from side to side, Eliana hoped she was a convincing liar. Never one for falsehood, Eliana couldn't help but break character and tell Kye an untruth. Their time together over the summer and fall, now into the winter, was more than just wasted time. She needed him.

Kye had spent nearly the last four years of his life saying goodbye to people. First his mom to the penal system, then his dad to God knows where, and countless foster parents and siblings. Eliana couldn't bear the thought of being another one. Mostly one for books and long walks alone, Eliana wasn't the poster child for friendship.

Raised as an only child by a father who spent more time working or drowning in a bottle, Eliana was painfully shy when she'd first met this dark-haired boy. Kye had given her something she'd never had: a steady place. This tumbleweed of a guy had rolled into her life, and she wasn't ready to let that go. How could she? In the late hours between studying, her mind had blissfully wandered to the idea that she and Kye could be more than friends. Were more than friends? They'd shared many a night planning their future to run away and join the circus, become stock-car drivers, even pirates if it meant getting out of Maine, their current lives, and on to better things. They had always been together since the first day they met. Why not now? Why couldn't Kye go to Massachusetts with her?

"Hey," Kye said gently as he noted the near look of panic on Eliana's face. He wrapped his arms around her and pulled her against him. "I don't want you to worry about that right now. Did you get accepted to Harvard?" She could only nod. "Then you'll find a way to get there. You're smart, Eli, the smartest person I've ever met. You can do anything!"

"You're sweet," she replied as she allowed him to hug her close. Resting his chin on the top of her head, Eliana missed the forlorn and somber expression that took over Kye's face. What he wouldn't do to give her the whole world, Harvard included. Sure, in his waking dreams he'd pictured them settled in a small house somewhere warm with a dog and seven children of their own. From the moment he'd met Eli, he knew she was never going to be happy with a small life. She deserved mansions and diamonds and a man who loved her more than alcohol. By God, he'd give it to her too.

No matter what.

HE'D BEEN at Hal's Garage for two weeks when he found himself limping down an alley in the business district of Pine Hill. Leaning behind a dumpster, he prayed the blood trail wasn't prominent enough to lead the shooter to his location.

Kye was struggling to settle his breathing. His heart was slamming in his chest like a jackhammer. Groaning in pain, he peeled the material of his pants away from his left thigh. Two blood stains—one on the front and the other on the back. Guessing it was a good sign of entry and exit wound, he pressed the back of his head against the building and forced himself to take several deep breaths.

The hospital was out of the question. They'd know instantly what kind of wound it was, and the last thing he needed was more cops or questions. His home with the Duncans was off the table. Part of their arrangement was a full bag check when he arrived home. A couple of religious sticklers, if they were going to confiscate a comic book they deemed inappropriate, they'd sure as hell notice a bullet wound.

Eliana…

Kye was limping forward before the thought had fully registered. His beautiful brown-eyed bestie was his only hope. He just prayed that at the late hour, it being nearly two in the morning, she was still awake.

Of course, she is. She's practically spent the last month pouring over Harvard.

Wasn't it her potential attendance that had landed him in this mess?

* * *

"Driscoll!" Dropping the socket wrench in his hand, Kye stood to his feet from his hunched position under the hood of a sedan and saw Hal waving him over. "Get in here!" he bellowed, his voice filling the entire shop like a loudspeaker. Kye wiped his hands on a rag as he moved toward the glass-walled office where Hal and another man were waiting. The stocky redheaded shop owner Kye was very familiar with, but the taller, gray-haired man dressed in head to toe leather was a complete stranger.

"You needed me, boss?"

"Close the door," Hal instructed as he sat behind his desk and lit a cigarette. He took a long drag while the door clicked shut and waved a hand at the taller man. "This is Max Strong," he said as though it was incredibly obvious. Taking the hint, Kye wiped his hand once more on his pants out of courtesy before shaking Max's hand.

"Nice to meet you, sir," Kye said politely. Max's imposing presence wasn't attested to his height alone. Probably pushing 6'5, the broad-shouldered man gave the impression that he commanded power and lots of it. His immaculately trimmed beard was a staunch gray that matched his hair perfectly, though Kye guessed he wasn't yet sixty. His eyes were a steely-silver and were definitely sizing him up.

"You don't know who I am," Max observed, his voice gravelly and deep. Kye only shook his head.

"Don't take that too harshly, Max, he's a foster. Been shacked up with the Duncans for a few months. We'll teach him what's what."

"Your parents dead?" Max asked shortly and looked between the two men.

"Possibly?"

"Just answer the question," Max instructed. Clearly, this was a man who wasn't going to take vagueness.

"Last I heard my mom was serving twenty-five to life in Timpanogos," Kye began as he stuffed his hands in his back pockets. "Haven't seen my dad since we lived in Utah."

"When was that?" Max asked, leaning against the far wall and lighting a cigarette. His brand had a much starchier smell than the sickly-sweet ones Hal smoked.

"About five years ago."

"He abandoned you?"

"Guess you could say that."

"Don't be coy, son," Max reprimanded, the lit end of his cigarette reflecting off his eyes and making them almost look red. Kye clenched his jaw. He didn't appreciate the interrogation. "What did I say about answering questions?"

"Well, we stopped at a rest stop halfway between Salt Lake City and Vegas. We stopped to take a piss, and when I came out of the bathroom his truck was gone. So, either he abandoned me, or he went on ahead to set up house."

"Watch your tone!" Hal snapped as he smacked the desk. Max was chuckling, though, his lips parting in a smile that revealed straight white teeth.

"Kid's got spunk," Max said to Hal.

"A bit too much," Hal mumbled.

"What's this about?" Kye asked, feeling he couldn't muster any more patience.

"Hal says you're not the smartest, but you're good with cars. Ever worked on bikes?"

"Ten-speed or beach cruiser?"

"Save the sarcasm, kid, it'll only get you a black eye," Max said calmly as he flicked ash from the tip of his cigarette.

"A few," Kye admitted.

"Where'd you learn?"

"Clark County."

"Juvie? How long?"

"Eight months."

"For?"

"Defacing city property," Kye said, crossing his arms. Max's heavy brow furrowed. "I punched a cop." Max erupted in loud and husky laughter. Even Hal let out a bark of amusement, and Kye couldn't help but grin along.

"What'd you do that for?" Max laughed as he wiped at his tears of amusement. Either that or the smoke-filled office was stinging his eyes the way it was Kye's.

"He hit me first."

"You got a temper or a death wish?" Max asked, putting out his cigarette in the ashtray on Hal's desk.

"Neither," Kye said with a shrug, "I just don't like assholes."

"Cops?"

"Like I said, assholes." Max laughed again and clapped a large hand on Kye's shoulder.

"Yeah, you were right, Hal. I like him." For a strange reason, Kye felt a sense of pride that he'd earned the approval of this man. "I got a proposition for you, kid. You fix up my bikes, clean 'em up real nice, I'll pay you and make you another offer. One that requires more discretion in what you store in the spoilers. Understand?"

"Yeah, I get it," Kye said, feeling this meeting had actually been an interview.

"The more offers I make, the better the money," Max stated as he began removing another light from the packet that he kept in the front pocket of his leather vest. "You wanna make some money, kid?"

"What if I say no?" Kye asked, his eyes darting back and forth again. Max's wide chest shook with quiet laughter. He took a long drag and blew it out, the plume hitting Kye in the face.

"You won't."

"COME ON, ELI," Kye whispered, feeling he was near passing out. He stood on her front lawn that was in desperate need of a mow, the soggy grass completely saturated after the onslaught of snow over Christmas had melted. Using a scrap of white shale from the broken lawn rocks framing the front walkway, Kye had been pelting the gutter above Eliana's window for almost ten minutes in hopes of drawing her attention.

At this time of night, it was likely her dad was in a whiskey sour coma, but Kye also knew that the man was more likely to be passed out on the couch in the living room just inside the front door. He could risk neither knocking nor ringing the bell. Having only met Eliana's dad once in the last eight months, the beer-bellied, heavy bearded man had made it clear that Kye wasn't welcome in his home or near his daughter.

"Kye?" Eliana asked as she'd pulled back her drapes and slid her window open. She could barely make out his silhouette in the moonlight. "What are you doing here?" she asked but couldn't keep the joy from her voice.

"Eli, I need your help; can you let me in?"

"What's wrong?"

"Please, just let me in."

"Meet me at the back door." She pulled her window closed, and Kye limped around the side of the house and felt hot tears prick at his eyes as he had to vault the chain-link fence. The back door to the house was at the top of a wooden deck, and Kye had to cling to the railing, using all the strength in his right leg to drag his left up the stairs.

"Hey," he said to Eliana who was waiting at the sliding glass door wrapped in a pink bathrobe and bare feet.

"Oh my God," she gasped when she saw his blood-soaked, light-wash jeans. "Kye, what happened?" she practically shrieked.

"Shh," he whispered and pushed past her to get inside and out of the cold. "I had an accident," he lied. "Do you have a first aid kit?"

"What kind of accident causes that much bleeding?" she asked skeptically as she took his hand and pulled him down the hall and into the upstairs bathroom. Turning on the light, Kye grimaced as the brightness hurt his eyes. He hadn't realized how exhausted and dehydrated he was. "Kye Driscoll, you answer me!" Eliana said as she helped him to lean on the counter. It was then she noticed he not only had a bleeding leg but a fat lip and red knuckles.

"It's not what you think," he said, sliding his arms out of his leather jacket. Fortunately for him, he'd had the thirty-minute walk to her house to think up his story. "I was putting in some overtime at Hal's; you know he's had a couple of big projects, and I wanted to impress him by getting it done early. I had a car jacked up on the lift, and I missed a step under the engine. Hit my head on the side of the pit, and the damn soldering iron went straight through my leg."

"Oh my God," she repeated. Her light brown eyes had gone wide during his recount, and now she was holding both sides of his face and examining his eyes. "Do you think you have a concussion?"

"No, I don't think so, but my head has felt better."

"Here," she said, grabbing a green hand towel from the rack and wetting it in the sink behind him. She gently pressed it to his lip, and Kye took it from her to hold it in place. "Why didn't you call 9-1-1?"

"I thought about it, but you know how Hal gets. He fired a guy last week for chipping the paint on a bumper. If he knew my clumsy ass had hurt myself on the job, I'd be fired for sure." Eliana could only nod. "Please, don't call an ambulance. I don't think it's too bad. I just need to get cleaned up."

"Alright," she relented. Her bottom lip had fit itself between her teeth, and Kye swallowed hard. "I'll get the kit, but you're going to need to lose those," she said, pointing to his pants. Kye felt heat rush to his face, and Eliana must have felt the same hot flash because her cheeks turned bright red. Without another word, she slipped from the bathroom and disappeared into the dark hall. He could hear her opening and closing doors somewhere out of sight.

"Aren't you worried about waking your dad?" he asked as he unbuckled his belt and dropped the fly.

"He's in Portland," she called back to him. "He and Uncle Ron are delivering a lumber shipment. They won't be back until tomorrow or the next day."

"Oh," Kye replied as his pants hit the tile floor, leaving him in a t-shirt and pair of blue boxers that were likely too tight for modesty. Using the same towel for his lip, he began wiping the blood from his thigh.

"Careful," Eli said from the doorway. "Cotton fibers can make the wound worse." She set the medical kit on the counter next to him. "Let me," she offered and sank to her knees. Tossing her hair out of her face, she wet a piece of gauze and began gently wiping the area around the wound.

Kye watched her with fascination as she tended to him. From his seated position, she was practically cradling his leg that was dusted with dark hair. Her long fingers didn't as much as tremble as she cleaned the blood and tossed the dirty bandages in the wicker garbage can. Her soft touch and the sight of her bobbing between his legs had him gripping the countertop.

"Ow!" he cried as she finally began dabbing at the hole in his leg.

"Sorry," she said sincerely and looked up at him. She

was biting her lip again. "It's only going to hurt for a moment." Shedding her bathrobe, she went back to work. Kye let himself be distracted from the pain by studying every inch of Eliana he could.

Her arms were left bare in her white tank top that fit her form perfectly. She was resting on her knees, and the top of her pajama pants had come down enough to show him a thin strip of skin on her lower back where he noted two dimples of the Venus that looked perfectly sized for his fingertips. With her hair pulled to the side, he could see the freckles from her neck stretching over her bare shoulder, and without thinking he brushed them with his thumb.

Eliana shivered when she felt his hand, but she continued to clean the lesion. "I don't think the rod went all the way through," she said in a breathy tone. "It looks like it just sliced right through the side."

"Hmm," came the sound from Kye. "Felt like it went straight through."

"Took a good chunk of skin, and there are burn marks," she noted, and his hand traveled from her shoulder to the side of her neck where his thumb brushed her jawline. "You're making it hard to focus," Eliana admitted as she tried to tape the thick bandage over the now cleaned abrasion.

"Am I?" Kye asked just as quietly. When she was finished, she'd paused, still in her kneeling position, until Kye used his hold on her neck to urge her to a stand. Still nestled between his legs, he got an excellent view of her braless chest that was rising and falling with short, rapid breaths. His fingertips trailed the line of her prominent collarbone, and her chills made her pearl-sized nipples perk up.

Eliana could hear the groaning sound from Kye's throat as he seemed to hesitantly appraise her. Sure, he'd seen her in a tank top before, countless times over the summer. Never so brazenly exposed, and definitely not when he was sitting in front of her with no pants on. Following his lead, she lifted her hand to touch his bicep. His tight grip on the counter made the muscles of his triceps stand out. His skin was warm. The muscles tightened under her touch, and he wrapped his arm around her to pull her against him.

Wordlessly, her eyes lifted to meet his, and the corner of his mouth turned upward as he saw her mercilessly chewing her bottom lip. After a moment of effort, he stood to his feet and used his free hand to take her chin. With a prod from his thumb, her teeth released her now plump lower lip, and he wasted no time taking her mouth with his.

Her soft moan made his grip on her waist tighten, and her arms wrapped around his neck to pull him closer. Though timid at first, Eliana felt her head swim and her toes curl at the sensation of his warm, soft lips that she knew she'd never get enough of. His fingertips were digging into her back, and hers were now raking through his hair. Pulling him closer by the back of the head, he suddenly broke the kiss and held her slightly away from him.

"What's the matter?" she asked abruptly. Kye pressed the back of his hand to his mouth, and she saw how swollen it had become.

"You bit me," he replied and laughed at her furious blush. She made to step away from him, but he pulled her back against him. "I don't mind," he whispered as he rested his forehead against hers. She smiled and splayed her hands on his chest.

"What took you so long?" she asked, trailing small circles with her fingers. Kye swallowed hard. Of course, he'd wanted to kiss her the moment he saw her. How could he, though? What did he have to offer the girl who was going to take over the world? When they'd met, he'd barely had the clothes on his back. Now, knowing he had a pocket full of cash, albeit bloodstained, thanks to Max there was a promise of a lot more to come. Maybe enough to afford Harvard.

"You know me, I'm a little thick," he teased, and she scowled at him. "Come here," he said, kissing her more gently this time. He earned himself another glorious moan, and he had to shift his weight, turning his hips away from her to avoid embarrassment. "I should go," he claimed as they parted.

"You can stay," Eliana offered, looking up at him with those wide, brown eyes that made him completely undone.

"Don't tempt me, Eli," Kye said, shaking his head and ducking to pull his pants on. Eliana felt the need to turn her back, but as she heard him buckling his belt, she looked back at him again. "It goes without saying, but thank you. I really owe you."

"Yeah you do," she agreed with a broad smile. He chuckled again and took a strand of her hair between his thumb and finger, giving it a soft tug. "I couldn't let you bleed to death, you're too cute." They'd moved to the back door, and he paused to brush her lips with his once more. "You're sure you don't want to stay? We've got a couch…"

"Eli, I'm going to need the walk home to cool off," he said with high eyebrows. Her bottom lip disappeared again, and he took her hand, kissing the back of it. "I'll see you, okay?"

"Okay…" He winked at her once before moving into the dark night. She watched him until he was out of sight and couldn't help but press her fingers to her lips that were still tingling euphorically.

3

———————

*E*liana was lying in bed wide awake when the sun came up. It cast a warm light through the curtains, and though the frigid January air hadn't relented its chill, Eliana felt impossibly and deliciously warm from head to toe. She'd tossed and turned most of the night, unable to quiet her mind enough to sleep. Her heart was still racing, and her stomach wouldn't sit still as if it were full of rocks. Kye had kissed her. Finally!

Tossing her blankets aside she rose, her bare feet hitting the cold wooden floors. She stood for a brief moment at the window, staring at the part of the lawn where she'd seen Kye only a few hours before. Her lips curved into a smile. Sitting on the soft chair in front of her vanity, Eliana began combing out her long hair.

Eliana's only goal in life had been to get out of Pine Hill as fast as possible. The town felt like the gutter drain of a dead-end alley to her. With the exception of a few joys, she'd lived a quiet and lonely life until she'd met Kye. He had blown into Pine Hill like the first warm breeze after a long winter bringing the promise of new life with him. The memory of their first exchange was still fresh in her mind.

"Pencils down," Mrs. King instructed from behind her desk. The clicking of writing utensils hitting desks mixed with sighs from the thirty students in the SAT Prep Class. Eliana was sitting center desk, front row, and she smiled at Mrs. King as the middle-aged woman with gorgeous red hair began collecting the exams. "Tomorrow we're going to focus on the essay writing portion for those of you who are in AP classes. For those who aren't, please be sure to bring your calculators as you'll be reviewing your math scores from today. Please take these worksheets home." Mrs. King handed Eliana the pile she knew she was instructed to pass out.

"Here," Eliana said, standing and turning to face the boy sitting behind her. He smiled up at her as he reached to take one.

'He has the most incredible blue eyes,' she mused. 'Blue like the sky on a summer day. Like ice on the Bering Sea...'

"Going to pass the rest out anytime today?" the sarcastic snap from Missy Deacon, the girl in the row next to her, startled Eliana from her thoughts. Blushing and ducking her head to break eye contact, she moved around the room to pass out the rest of the worksheets. When she was finished and returning to her desk, she passed in front of Missy who thought it hilarious to stick one perfectly manicured foot out and trip her. The gaggle of girls burst into laughter, and Eliana tumbled into her desk and nearly onto the floor.

"Missy, that's enough!" Mrs. King snapped as she placed a hand on Eliana's arm. "Are you alright?" Eliana only nodded as she slid into her desk and adamantly avoided the look the boy behind her was casting her way. She was beyond embarrassed. Nervously fiddling with her braid, the one she was sure to weave her hair into since the first day of Prep, she waited for the teacher to hand her quiz back from the day before. "Good job, Eliana," Mrs. King said, setting the paper in front of her.

"Thank you," Eliana said and managed a smile. She'd gotten a perfect score on her grammar and writing! A cough that sounded suspiciously like 'teacher's pet' caused another round of giggles from the girls to her right. "What's your problem, Missy?" Eliana asked the blonde who was glaring at her.

"I don't have a problem," she cooed with a brief glance at the dark-haired boy, "but now that you mention it..."— she made an exaggerated sniffing noise as she leaned toward Eliana— "do you smell alcohol?"

The girls laughed mercilessly, and Eliana felt angry tears well up.

"What did you get on your exam, Missy?" the bold voice of the boy behind her cut through the laughter. Without waiting for a response, he grabbed the paper off Missy's desk and looked it over. "Wow, Missy…" He sighed. "At least you spelled your name correctly. Oh, wait, no… you spelled 'Bitch' wrong." The entire class, including Eliana, erupted in laughter, and the blonde turned beet red.

"That's enough, that's enough!" Mrs. King called over the raucous. "You have your tests and your homework, I'll see you all tomorrow." Students began filing from the room, and Missy made a point of shoving Eliana's backpack off her desk as she left.

"Classy," Eliana muttered as she knelt to gather the books and papers that had scattered to the floor.

"Ignore her," the boy said as he helped gather her things.

"I've been ignoring her since second grade," Eliana replied with a bitter chuckle. "Thanks," she said, standing and taking the book he was handing her. "Thanks for what you said. I've never been the best at confrontation," Eliana admitted.

"You? I can't imagine!" His exaggerated tone was teasing, and she couldn't help grinning. "I'm Kye."

"Eliana." He took her outstretched hand, their eyes met, and they both smiled.

With a wistful sigh, Eliana commemorated the memory by braiding her hair in a fishtail and moved to her closet to dress for the day. Never one for the flashier styles, Eliana preferred to dress simply. Her closet was full of mostly earth tones and items easily layered.

She was still pulling on her sweater when she heard the crash from downstairs. Racing from her room, her feet pounded down the stairs, and she saw her father collapsed on the floor in front of the door. He was a massive man, broad-chested and full-bellied with a bald head and thick brown beard. He was still wearing his work overalls, and his hardhat, having fallen from his head, was spinning in circles in the doorway to the kitchen.

"Dad!" She sighed as he attempted to crawl to his feet. The paper sack he'd been carrying had ripped, and several bottles now lay broken on the floor. "Be careful, you'll cut yourself," she scolded as he tried to scoop up the remains. Despite his portly stature, he looked like a small child who had spilled his crayons.

"Help me, Liana," he groaned as he tried to scoot the liquid into a broken half of a bottle, "get me a cup or something. I don't want to waste any."

"Dad, come on," she said as she placed a hand on his stooped back. "I'll take care of this," she assured him.

"Let's get you up to bed." He struggled a moment to stand all the way up and began licking the liquid off his hand.

"Wait, wait," he said and grabbed one of the bottles that were still intact. "One out of three is better than none."

"Dad!"

"It's alright, I'm alright," he declared as he moved toward the stairs. He tucked the bottle under one arm and draped his other over Eliana's shoulder as she practically dragged him up the stairs.

"I thought you and Uncle Ron were gone for a few more days," she asked with discomfort. By the smell of him, he'd been back a while, and he'd stopped at the pub for a few before coming home.

"If anyone asks, we're still out of town," Henry instructed as he stumbled down the hall and into his bedroom which was past Eliana's.

"Why?"

"Don't ask that, Liana. We were gone the last two days and we're gone two days more, under-understand? We-we already got paid for four days on the road, and I'm not returning none of the money!"

"Dad, you're going to get in trouble if you keep fudging numbers at work..."

"Who's fudging?" he roared and pushed himself off

her only to stumble into the wall. "We delivered all the wood we were supposed to!"

"You had six stops as far north as Ellsworth, how did you do that in two days?"

"You're not the only one with brains," he said, tapping his temple for emphasis. He swayed for a moment, and she had to catch him before he fell.

Eliana sighed as she helped him sit on the bed. He had unscrewed the lid to the bottle and took a long drink of whiskey, the smell of which made her gag before he smiled up at her. Droplets of alcohol were dripping from his scruffy beard. "I need to go clean up the glass before I'm late for school." Before she moved, he grabbed her hand.

"How did I get so lucky to have a saint for a daughter?" he asked, his bloodshot eyes closing as he rocked back.

With an even heavier sigh, Eliana answered, "You married an angel who gave birth to a saint." Her reply sounded as rehearsed as it was.

"That's right, your mother, she was an angel. Only an angel like her could give me a saint like you," Henry said dreamily as he curled up on the bed cradling his bottle like an infant.

"Get some sleep, Dad, I'll see you tonight." She kissed him on the top of the head and closed the door behind her as she left. Mustering up memories of Kye, she tried to force herself into a good mood as she descended the stairs to begin mopping up the liquid demon that lay on the floor of the foyer.

Cleaning up the broken glass was easy enough, but when she knelt to wipe up the alcohol, she felt the tears rolling down her face and dripping onto the floor. It wasn't the fact that she was cleaning up his drunken mess; it was the fact she was so used to it that brought on the sudden emotion.

For years Eliana had prided herself on her stoicism, never letting anything get her too riled up. Growing up without a mom? Others had done it. Bullied in school? Just ignore them. Didn't have any friends? Studying was a constant companion. Dad forgot to pay the bills and came home drunk again? Time for a second job. No sweat, no fuss, no mess.

Maybe today it was the lack of sleep over the last week. Or the stress of her impending graduation. Or maybe it was the fact that only hours before she'd felt the most joy she'd felt in her entire life in the arms of the boy she was falling in love with, only to be dragged back down to reality with the crash of a whiskey bottle. The dramatic shift in emotions was enough to splinter her resolve.

Throwing the towels into the laundry, Eliana peeled her clothes off. The last thing she wanted was to go to school smelling like alcohol. Lord knew Missy would notice. Grabbing a green sweater from the closet, she swapped out her tank top and jeans from the top drawer of her dresser where her eyes landed on a portrait of her mother.

If there were any other photos of Gwendolyn in the house, they were kept under lock and key. This was the only one she'd ever seen, and Eliana had only managed to find it when she'd been cleaning out their basement after it had flooded three years ago. It had been stored in an old baby book of Eliana's that had been too saturated with murky water to be salvaged. Fortunately, the photograph was tucked inside a plastic cover and had been mostly undamaged. Only the edges were slightly discolored and the water stains weren't enough to dim the beautiful woman's brilliance.

Her mother had always seemed like a fairy tale. Some distant, perfect, impossible to be real heroine her father rarely spoke about but idolized magically. The photograph was of Gwen posing for the camera holding a small, pink bundle she knew was herself only days after being born. Her mother's hair was wild and glowed with sunlight. Face completely devoid of makeup, her lazy smile and half-lidded eyes spoke volumes of her fatigue but also her ease. She looked so natural. Gwen would have made an excellent mother if she'd had the chance.

In perfect irony, alcohol had robbed her of both

parents. First, her mother nearly thirteen years prior in a drunk driving accident and then her father after he'd crawled in a bottle and never came out. Eliana hated alcohol. It was a hate that permeated every cell in her. Though she'd never taken a single drop, she felt it constricting every moment of her life since her mother had died. Escape was her only option.

Turning from the photo, Eliana made her way to the desk next to her bed. It was covered in papers and sketches and letters of all kinds. The most prominent was a brochure for Harvard University and her acceptance letter with a certificate of scholarship. They sat right next to a map of the town surrounding the school and circled in red was the apartment she'd reserved and put down payment on. It had taken half her savings account, but she'd paid six months of rent on the one bedroom, one bathroom, mother-in-law apartment in a boarding house. It was hers.

Kye's too, if he wanted it.

Putting nearly as much research into planning their future as she did her application, Eliana had managed to find and secure lodging as well as a job waiting tables starting that summer. She'd even spoken to three local auto shops that had agreed to interview Kye if he wanted a job. He could work during the day when she was in classes. She could wait tables in the evening and weekends, and in their free time they could be together.

Kye could even try for junior college if he wanted! All her education had paid off. She'd planned the perfect life for them together.

With time running out before Kye was too old for foster care aide, she knew he was going to need somewhere to live after the Duncans. Why not with her? Eliana had sworn to herself she wouldn't mention a word of it to him until she was certain of his feelings. Call it the pains of life, but she'd learned to be guarded. Knowing her own heart was on the line unless she was certain he cared for her the way she cared for him, how could she possibly propose they live together? Even as friends?

Now she knew. The way he'd come to her when he needed help. The way he'd held on to her like she was priceless to him. The way he'd kissed her… she knew— he was falling in love with her too.

If her mother was a fairy tale princess, Pine Hill was the tower Eliana felt trapped in, then the hero of the story was Kye. Her Knight in Shining Armor.

More importantly— he was hers.

4

"You were out late last night," Stanley Duncan said over the top of his newspaper as Kye, his eldest foster son, entered the kitchen. Stan was an older man in his mid-sixties with a dusk of white hair that created a perimeter around the bald top of his head. He was short, well under six foot, and he used his retirement from accounting to help his wife run her craft store.

"Transmission fell out of Mr. Grouper's minivan," Kye said, grabbing a piece of bacon off the plate on the counter. "I told Hal I'd stay until it was done."

"You know curfew is ten on a school night," Stan continued and folded his paper before setting it down.

"What was I supposed to do, leave early? I promised Hal," Kye argued.

"You also promised to follow house rules," Carey,

Stan's wife, chimed in from her position in front of the frying pan on the stove. Just as petite, the round woman had a mop of white and blonde highlighted hair. "Next time you need to call…"

"There won't be a next time, will there?" Stan interrupted. Kye sat opposite Carey on one of the stools, and she handed him a glass of orange juice.

"Listen, I don't mean any disrespect to you guys," Kye began, "you've been great, really, but I'm eighteen in like two weeks. I haven't broken a single house rule since I got here. I've got a good job, and we all know that I need to have a plan for when I age out. If Hal asks me to work late, I'm going to stay."

"Well," Stan said, folding his hands and looking at his wife before replying, "I can't say I agree with everything you said, but you make a valid point. You've been well-behaved and hard-working these last eight months. Just don't work too hard…"

"Please call or text if you're going to be out past midnight," Carey added as she set a plate of food in front of him. "You know Stan worries," she said with a wink.

"I will, thanks," he said and downed a few mouthfuls of eggs before sliding out of his chair and grabbing his coat.

"Leaving already?" Carey asked with surprise.

"I want to walk Eli to school, I need to get a head start."

"In sweatpants?" she asked with hands on hips. Kye only shrugged and set his plate in the sink. "See you tonight then."

"Yeah okay," he called over his shoulder as he made to leave.

"Kye," Stan called, and Kye resisted an annoyed sigh as he turned to look back at the pair. Carey standing with her hand on her husband's shoulder, staring at him with rounded eyes. "Whether seventeen, eighteen or thirty-five you're welcome in this house."

Kye could only manage a nod, a sudden lump in his throat, before closing the door behind him as he left. Of all the foster homes he'd been in, he was most grateful for the Duncans. Stan's comment about being welcome gave Kye a small feeling of guilt that he'd lied. As much as he would have loved to walk Eliana to school, his leg was killing him. It was going to take the extra thirty minutes just to get to school on time.

Though admittedly not one to rush for academics, he was in more of a hurry this morning than any before. He couldn't wait to see Eliana. Just the thought of seeing her again, kissing her again, made the pain in his leg more bearable.

Though his plans were cut short. Only six blocks from school, he heard an all too familiar rumble approach. Turning around he saw four motorcycles, Max's chopper in the lead, pull up next to him. Kye shifted his backpack onto the other shoulder as Max pulled the facemask off his mouth and took off his sunglasses.

"Get on," he instructed shortly. Looking at the other four men he recognized as Wayne, Hamilton, Riggs, and Shon, Kye knew it wasn't a request. These might as well have been the Four Horsemen of the Apocalypse.

Kye took the spare helmet off the sissy bar and slid onto the bike. With a roar, they peeled off.

* * *

PINE HILL WASN'T a large town. Two main roads, a grand total of one stop light, a hardware store, two diners, a gas station, an arcade a bowling alley, three bars and a grocery store made up the downtown district. The majority of the town was divided into two industrial yards: one lumber mill and the other an old train depot that was renovated into a scrap metal yard.

A warehouse and six adjoined shipping containers made up the headquarters of Screaming Demons. Their black, silver and blue tags were littered on every broad wall and a chain-link fence penned in their accommodations.

Max and the others pulled to a stop at the main hall, and they all dismounted. Wordlessly following their leader, they stepped inside. The wide-open room had a makeshift bar and kitchenette with fold-out tables lined up for dining. On the other side of the room was a large TV with three worn-out couches and a few armchairs that were covered in cigarette burns. There were at least a dozen men strewn about, some working on bikes in the open space, a few watching television, and others shooting pool.

"Get him a beer," Max said to Wayne as they sat at the bar that was constructed from crates and tin siding. Wayne, a tall bald man with tattoos on both arms, opened the glass door refrigerator and retrieved two Coors then set them in front of both men. "Heard about last night," Max said, taking a long drink.

"I figured you would," Kye admitted as he wiped condensation from the bottle.

"You wanna tell me what happened?" Max wasn't looking directly at him, but his profile was just as intimidating. Combined with Wayne leaning against the opposite wall staring at him, and Riggs and Hamilton just behind them, Kye felt surrounded.

"We went to the bridge like you asked," Kye started. "Grier and I were ten miles on the New Hampshire side waiting to escort the truck, and the rest of the guys were on the home side waiting to relieve us. Three in, six out, just like you asked."

"So, what went wrong?"

"Grier and I got nervous; the truck was late by

almost an hour. I told Grier to wait while I looked ahead to see what the hold-up was. I wasn't five minutes down the road when I saw the box truck pulled off to the side with its hazards on. I called Grier to tell the others to meet me down the road. While I waited, I checked out the truck. The cabin was empty, tires weren't flat, and doors were left open. When I went around to the back, the roll-up door was open, but the cargo was intact."

"What exactly did you see?"

"I climbed inside and there were the car parts, the ceramic crates with the hash, and wheel rims. Everything was there."

"Everything?" Max asked and finally turned to fully face Kye. Max's set jaw was the only inclination he needed to know this was a very serious conversation.

"I didn't steal anything if that's what you're asking. Everything I was told would be in the truck was there." Max eyed him for a moment then gestured for him to continue his story. "That's when I heard the sirens. It was one set of blues, but I figured I'd better haul ass before they got there. I hopped out and moved the bike behind the tree-line when I heard someone moving around in the woods. Next thing I know there are gunshots. I got hit once, but I managed to get back to the truck and start it up. I didn't look back, I just drove. Ten minutes later I was over the bridge with the others.

I gave Grier the truck and made my way through town on foot."

"Who shot at you, the blue?" Max asked with his arms crossed.

"I don't think so; the squad car hadn't reached us yet. He must have been county, though, because he didn't follow me if he was looking for the truck. I knew that Grier would have a better shot at losing a tail than I would which is why I swapped him spots."

"Grier knows the safe roads," Max agreed. "What about the bike I lent you?" Kye dropped his eyes. "Still in the woods?"

"I didn't get it behind the trees… It was still on the side of the road."

"So, it's in police custody then."

"Do we know that for sure?"

"They were looking for the truck, I have no doubt about that. They would have been looking in that area. It's right on the county and state line."

"I'm sorry, Max, I made the call to jump in the truck when I was getting shot at."

"Did you see who was shooting?"

"Yeah, sort of. It was some guy. No cut, so I don't think it was another gang. Tall, bigger guy, real trucker looking."

"He alone?"

"I don't know. Bullets started flying, and I hauled ass.

Could have been more, but I didn't see any. Listen, I'll pay you back for the bike. I'll work it off…" Max held up his hand to quiet him. Using two fingers, he waved for him to follow, and they crossed the room to the back of the warehouse. Kye could feel his palms starting to sweat.

"You said you were hit," Max stated as they entered the back hallway. "You go to the hospital?"

"No, no, I knew better than that. I, uh… patched myself up. Just grazed my leg."

"Bet it hurts like a bitch," Max said as he opened the door to outside where a large circle of men, all in Screaming Demon cuts, were standing. Kye froze. Max clamped a hand on the back of Kye's neck and urged him forward. "You shoulda had that beer, kid, this isn't going to feel good." Shoving him into the center of the circle, the men descended.

Kye didn't even have a chance to defend himself as each man took a turn throwing a punch. The first two were to his abdomen, the third took a cheap shot to his kidneys, but the fourth to his nose put him on his back. A kick to the wound in his leg made him cry out.

"Pick him up," Max ordered, and two men grabbed each arm. Kye was bleeding from the nose, and he could feel his right eye swelling. Max stood in front of him and removed his leather jacket then handed it to another Demon. "You went on ahead to scout out the truck without backup, entered the cargo hold of a truck you knew had stolen parts and drugs without authorization, fled from a gunfight after getting yourself shot and left an unmarked bike on the scene…" Max cracked his knuckles before landing a powerful uppercut. "A bike with no plates, manufactured entirely of stolen parts, with no VIN. You risked all driving that truck back over state lines with a badge on your tail. You know what we do with guys like that?"

Kye was in no condition to answer as he hung limp between the two men who were now dragging him through the dirt toward the floodlights. He managed to lift his head, expecting to see himself at the wrong end of a gun; instead, he saw Max with his hand resting on the handle of a mint condition Shadow Chopper with the Screaming Demon emblem on the side.

"What do we do with guys like that?" Max asked again as he singlehandedly lifted Kye to his feet and clamped a jacket over his shoulder. "We recruit him," he finished. "Welcome to the family, son."

5

"Kye, this is ridiculous," Eliana protested as Kye urged her forward as he stood behind her with one hand on her upper arm and the other over her eyes. "I've got midterms to study for…"

"Snooze!" Kye yelled and for dramatic effect let out a snoring noise. "You've been holed up in the library for two days. At this rate, you've got the entire calculus section memorized."

"I was studying history today, actually."

"Even more boring. You need a break." Kye removed the hand on her arm and opened a door in front of them. A waft of smoke and the smell of floor polish hit them, and Eliana laughed, knowing already where they were. "Tada!"

"Bowling?" she asked with mirth as she saw several patrons already at play.

"Not just bowling," he said, holding up a mesh bag of gold tokens. "We've got enough tokens for a dozen games of whack-a-gator and skee ball. Both of which, I intend on demolishing you in."

"You think so?" Eliana asked with a grin as she placed both hands on her hips. "I'll have you know, Kye Driscoll, that whether bowling or skee I'm pretty savvy with handling balls." Kye burst into laughter and at Eliana's confused face began laughing even harder.

"Eli," he said, slinging an arm around her shoulders, "I would love for you to show me how good you are with balls."

"Are you being dirty?" she asked, elbowing him.

"Entirely."

Kye was sitting on his new motorcycle in front of the gas station caddy-cornered to the park, and he was twirling an arcade token between his knuckles. He looked up as he saw Eliana enter the playground, clearly having walked from the direction of their school. She took a seat on one of the swings where they always waited for each other. From his position behind one of the gas pumps and with his helmet still on, he knew there was little to no chance of her seeing him. He needed it that way.

Kye had needed to skip school the last few days. The beating he'd taken as part of his initiation had left him with several bruises and a cracked rib that were definitely going to be noticed. Students would talk, teachers would ask questions, and six days shy of his birthday he wasn't about to ruin his chances of making a clean break from the institution. Even if that meant he hadn't seen Eliana in person since their kiss.

That was agony.

She was wearing a white sweater and black jeans. She wore a bright red wool hat with two braids sticking out the bottom. She was looking around, clearly searching for him, and Kye pulled the blue bandana around his neck over his mouth for an extra layer of cover. Her head dropped, and he saw her fishing in her pocket. He felt a buzzing in his back pocket and removed his cell.

'Where are you?' lit up on his text message screen. 'I'm freezing.'

'Sorry to keep you waiting, El.'

'It's okay. Meet me in the tree? I have a surprise I wanted to talk to you about.'

'Can you text it to me?'

'I'd rather talk in person.'

'I hate to let you down. I can't make it.'

'Why not?'

'I got wrapped up at the garage.'

'I can stop by.'

'I'm out running errands. I don't know when I'll be back.' Kye waited, expecting her to text right back.

When she didn't, he looked up to see she was already leaving the park and heading home. 'Hey, I'm really sorry.' She paused in her retreat to reply.

'If you're avoiding me I wish you'd just tell me.' It took all of his self-restraint not to run across the street to her.

'El, I'm not avoiding you...' Even as he typed it he knew he was lying. Wasn't he avoiding her? His face was six shades of purple, and he was now brandishing a Screaming Demons cut. 'There's something I want to talk to you about too. I promise, I'll come find you soon. Just trust me. I want you back in my arms ASAP.' He could see just from her posture that she was smiling.

'I want that too.' His heart flipped. 'Don't take too long.'

'I won't. I'll make it up to you in all sorts of ways.'

'Kye Driscoll, don't you be dirty with me.'

Before he could type in his response, the bell over the gas station door rang loudly, and Grier exited with a plastic sack in one hand, his helmet in another, and a piece of beef jerky hanging out of his mouth.

"What's that?" Grier muttered through his mouthful, and Kye quickly pocketed his phone.

"Nothing," he lied, "just seeing if we got an update from Max."

"We won't," Grier said, tearing the meat in half, "he's gone to church."

"Church? Didn't take him for a religious man." Grier laughed and smacked Kye on the shoulder.

"So young, so much to learn," he teased, and Kye swatted his hand away as Grier pinched his cheek. "Church is when patched members of the Screaming Demons discuss business; however, today, all chapters of the Screaming Demons are meeting."

"How many chapters are there?"

"I'm not entirely sure. Three, at least. One in Maine, obviously," Grier stated as he straddled his own bike, "One in Massachusetts and the other in West Virginia. Max keeps in regular contact with them. Rumor has it we'll be doubling our transport of packages along the coast."

"Max acted really strange when we were talking about the cargo from the truck," Kye said and accepted a piece of dried meat from his companion. "He almost sounded like some items were missing. What do we deal?"

"Whatever sells," Grier answered as he strapped his helmet on. "Guns, opioids, car parts mostly."

"I didn't see any guns in the truck…"

"That must have been what the driver made off with," Grier concluded. "Whoever jumped you probably came back for the rest, or he was too dumb to haul ass when he had the chance."

"Why weren't we driving the truck, you know, one of us?"

"You kidding?!" Grier called. "Max never puts one of his own behind the wheel. We always deal with third parties. Keeps things clean. If they're busted, and it's happened, they can't ever trace the package to us. Besides, that driver was hired by the Vermont chapter. Probably why Max called Mass today."

"I feel sorry for the asshole who gets the blame," Kye stated before they both started up their bikes.

"Don't, whoever fucked up the deal deserves what they get. Max runs a perfect operation, has ever since he founded the club twenty years ago. You and me, we just keep our heads down, mouths shut, and tanks full. We'll be rich before too long."

"Speaking of which, let's get that package to the border. I got some stuff to buy," Kye said, smiling.

"Aww, baby boy," Grier chided, "with your ugly mug, no amount of money is going to buy you a hooker."

"Shut up," Kye retorted with an eye roll, and he pulled out of the station.

"Maybe a really ugly one!" Grier yelled after him. "My sister is single!"

ELIANA TRIED NOT to let disappointment overwhelm her, but having gone three days without seeing Kye she was losing faith. Her expectation after their kiss was that they'd be closer than ever, but since that night they hadn't been in the same room.

At school, they didn't share any classes except afternoon study hall. Kye was in standard courses, two of which were remedial because of all his transfers. Eliana had technically finished all her required classes to graduate and was taking three prep courses and two running start classes. It was likely she'd still have to take them in her first years of college, but any bit of a head-start she could get she was going to take.

They usually ate lunch together on the bench outside of the cafeteria, and then spent sixth period in the library before hanging out after school, but alas, Kye was either skipping school altogether or wasn't frequenting their usual spots. Either way, she missed him. His absence reminded her too much of her life before they'd met. Lonely.

Grabbing the mail from the box before entering the house, Eliana could already sense her dad had finished his stash of bottles and was looking for more because the house was in complete disarray. Knowing that his daughter usually poured out whatever she could find, Henry took to hiding his bottles in the couch cushions, in the closet, in drawers with dishes or cupboards.

"What have you done, Eliana?" he snapped as he slammed a drawer in the kitchen shut. Eliana set her backpack on the round dining table and tossed the mail next to it.

"I haven't done anything, Dad," she said, feeling a headache coming on.

"Oh yes, you have," Henry bellowed as he came around the kitchen island and stood in her face. "I saw the empty bottles in the garbage! Those cost money, you know!"

"First of all, the bottles in the garbage are the ones you broke when you got home, and secondly, I know full well that a bottle of cheap whiskey from Norm's costs $6.99 because not only have you sent me there to buy them for you, but you've managed to buy and drink so many bottles you forgot to pay the gas bill—again!" She slammed the yellow enveloped bill against her dad's chest before moving into the kitchen to start closing cabinet doors. Eliana's temper was getting the best of her, and when she got this angry she preferred to be left alone.

"I don't care for that tone, young lady. I'm your father, and you'll show me some respect!" He was snapping at her all the while opening the letter and scanning the overdue amount with his eyes.

"Being angry at you doesn't mean I'm disrespectful, it

means I'm sick of this argument. I'm tired of drinking being the only thing that matters to you!"

"That's what you think, is it?" He rounded on her and took hold of her arm painfully. "You think I wake up at three in the morning to go into work for booze? No, I go for you! To provide for you! I've been raising you by myself since your mother died."

"Tell me something I don't already know." Her breath caught in her throat as Henry raised his fist to backhand her, but he stopped himself short.

"That's a warning," he said, pointing at her. "You don't talk to your father like that." Eliana could think of a million things she wanted to say; instead, she bit her tongue so forcefully that she could taste blood. Henry's face softened, and he placed both of his hands on her shoulders. "Listen I-I'm going to pay the water bill…"

"Gas bill."

"That one too, okay, don't you worry about anything. You just study real hard and keep chasing your dream of getting into Harvard, and I'll take care of everything." His sentimental sincerity made Eliana feel momentarily sorry for him. Henry was as much a slave to the bottle as the bottle was to him.

"I got in," she muttered.

"What?"

"I got in. I was accepted. I was on the wait list for

months, but a few others had dropped so… I got in. I'm going to Harvard in the fall."

"My Liana is going to Harvard?" Henry asked in breathy awe. "My baby girl!" He wrapped his branch-like arms around and hoisted her into a bear hug. "You did it! Harvard! That's wonderful!" He swung her around, and Eliana had to squirm for a minute before he set her down. "My little saint, we've done it," he praised as he held her face in both hands. Eliana felt increasingly uncomfortable. "I'm so proud."

"Thanks, Dad."

"Come on, let's go celebrate! Let's get ice-cream! We'll go to Joan's Diner and get hot fudge sundaes with extra cherries like we used to when you were little. Remember your first report card with all A's? We ate so much ice-cream I got sick. Remember?"

"Yeah, Dad," she replied, but clearly his memory wasn't as good as hers. Henry hadn't gotten sick off too much ice-cream, he'd gotten sick because after two sundaes he'd gone to the bathroom, taken a detour at the bar next door, and after an hour of searching, Eliana had found him with two of his work buddies who were sporting seven empty glasses between them. "I'm not much for ice-cream these days."

"No?" he asked and looked a little dejected. "Okay, well… I'll just go pick something up. Yo-you clean the kitchen, and I'll bring something home for dinner. Burgers? Fries? Want a milkshake?"

"Sure, Daddy," Eliana said, feeling she needed to humor his momentary need to be a real dad. "Can you get vani-"

"Vanilla, yes, your favorite! See, I know my daughter!" he congratulated himself. Kissing her on the forehead, he discarded the urgent piece of mail, and left through the front door. Eliana watched from the window above the kitchen sink as he stumbled into the driver's seat of his blue truck and backed out of the driveway.

"He won't be back tonight," she admitted to herself and turned on the hot water to fill the right side of the sink. With a little dish soap, she began scrubbing the dishes that had piled up over the last few days.

Letting out one long and forlorn sigh, Eliana forced her mind to her 'happy place' as she called it. She imagined the day she got on the bus to leave, how it would drive across the one bridge that led in and out of town. Promising herself to not look back, not even once, she'd never return to Pine Hill. She'd make a beautiful home of her new apartment that would be full of plants and books and maybe even a fish. She'd never owned a pet before. Eliana imagined herself sitting in the lecture hall of her pre-law class. She'd sit in the center of the room, dressed in a Harvard sweatshirt, and she'd raise her hand to answer all the questions.

Looking at her hands that were covered in soapy bubbles, Eliana sighed again but with much more optimism. Maybe one day she'd be standing over a sink like this in a house of her own, washing dishes her children had dirtied. They would never grow up without a mother, with an alcoholic father, going to school smelling like booze and stale cigarettes. They'd laugh and dance and smile, read and imagine, and they'd love each other.

Maybe one day Eliana would look down at her hands and see a simple but beautiful wedding ring given to her by a man who loved her above everything and everyone else. He'd be handsome and kind, he'd make her laugh more than cry, and he'd hold her like he never wanted to let go.

The way Kye had held her…

6

Grier and Kye were still laughing and shoving each other's shoulders when they entered the clubhouse. They'd returned from a weekend away on business and based on their ear-to-ear grins it had clearly been a success.

The Demon's Den was still bustling with their out of town chapters who'd attended church earlier that week. While they were busy preparing to depart, they would likely spend another two or three nights in Maine before leaving.

"Boys," Max greeted from his seat at a round table. He held a fat cigar in one hand and a deck of cards in the other. A bleach blonde with hardly any clothing on her voluptuous body was draped over his lap like a doll. The two other men at the table were the chapter seniors,

Simon "Red Dog" Kratz from Vermont and "Nickels" from West Virginia.

"Boss," Grier greeted and stood to Max's left.

"Sing me a song," Max instructed without looking up from his deck.

"Went off without a hitch, boss," Grier began. "We met with the dealers in Waterville and Lewiston. Got in good with the distributors who work the streets. We got them to agree for resale at fifteen percent."

"What?" Max asked and in his surprise, he nearly dropped his cards and the woman on his lap. "No legit dealer is going to distribute for less than twenty-five, who the hell did you meet with?" Max had forgone his hand of cards for a fist full of Grier's shirt.

"Max, it was with the guys you set up! Honest!" Grier said, his usually tawny face a stark pale now. "Ask Kye, he knows! He was the one who got the discount." Max looked between the two younger boys for a moment before releasing Grier. With a shift in his chair, the blonde got the hint and stood, her long legs carrying her toward the bar but not before she cast one last look back at Kye. She offered him a flirtatious wink while she was at it.

"That true?" Max asked, drawing Kye's attention back. "Boy, you'd better have one good story for me. I don't like it when plans go awry."

"Grier and I had double-timed it to Lewiston. Grier has been teaching me some maneuvers on the bike, how to look for side roads, you know? In case you ever need an extra driver…" Max waved his hand impatiently. "So when we got there we decided to fish around, see if there was any competition with other suppliers. Heard rumor around one of the campuses that some recent manufacturers were diluting their last batches. When we met with the dealers from the west side, we used that as leverage."

"How?"

"They were sick of inflation, so they insisted on trying the goods before buying," Grier added.

"That's insulting," Max said, rapping a knuckle on the table.

"That's what Kye said," Grier continued. "He played it cool, though, let them try a gram. Even offered to buy out all their diluted stock while they thought over the decision." Max gave Kye an angry look, but before he could say anything Kye chimed back in.

"What the west side didn't know was that we were already meeting with the north and east who jumped at the offer. We gave them their bulk order at sixty-percent the cost with the understanding they were not to cross territories or buy from their old manufacturers, and they had to surrender their old stock."

"So, we got the monopoly in two territories?"

"Three," Grier added excitedly. "South side heard

about our offer and jumped at it. By the time west side came around, they were iced out of every district and had no back stock. Kye charged them double the price for half the supplies. They had no choice but to agree."

"Ha!" Max exclaimed, slamming his hand on the table, the colored poker chips rattling. "That'll teach 'em to question our quality."

"It gets better," Grier practically shouted. "They were so desperate to keep up with the other districts, they put down payment on the next four months of purchase plus ten percent if we sell to them first. Word spread to Watertown we were driving a hard bargain, and they straight up offered over our asking price to ensure business."

"What about the diluted drugs?"

"We dropped them at our warehouse. Roz said he could melt them down, filter them, and have them ready for redistribution in a week or so," Kye finished.

"Boys, you did damn good," Max said proudly as he stood and placed a fatherly hand on each of their shoulders. "Here I thought I'd sent you on a typical recon, but you surprised me. Get your bikes to the shop to get cleaned up. I'm going to think up a fat reward for you two." Grier was quick to race off, but Kye was halted by Max's strong hand still on his shoulder. "I'm proud of you, son. You've done well this last month with us. Never thought Hal could tell his own face from the ass-end of a dog, but he sure saw talent in you."

"Thanks, Max," Kye said sincerely. Whether he'd admit it to himself or not, he was eager for the approval of the hulking man.

"Why don't you meet me in the bunker after you drop your gear off? I have a surprise for you." Kye only nodded before heading out front. It only took him a few minutes to get his bike to the shop and retrieve his backpack. The first thing he did was pull out his cell phone and send off a quick text.

Back from my college visit, beautiful. Can't wait to see you.

He had just entered the bunker where a few extra bedrooms were located for those who chose to sleep over or were too drunk to leave when he got her reply.

Meet me at the tree?

Knowing his foster parents weren't expecting him until later, Kye was ready to send his reply when a hand pulled him into the closest room.

"What the…" His words were cut off by a set of red lips pressed against his. After a moment of standing in shock, he pushed the person off and flicked on the light. Standing in front of him, in nothing but a bra and jean shorts, was the blonde from before. "I think you got the wrong room," Kye said and began opening the door.

"Oh no, I'm in the right place." She laughed and

closed the door with a firm push of her hand. Kye turned and got a full face view of her chest as she pinned her hands on either side of him.

"Shouldn't you be looking for Max?" he asked, feeling blood rush in his ears.

"Who do you think sent me?" she asked, trailing a manicured finger down his chest. "Surprise," she teased, and Kye felt his face pale as she started kissing his neck.

"Listen, I'm, uh… flattered, but no thanks," he stuttered as he took her by the arms and held her at a distance. Her ruby red lips pursed into a pout, and she must have had something in her eye the way her lashes started fluttering.

"You don't like me?"

"I have a girl."

"Oh, is that all?" she said, laughing and wrapping her arms around his neck. "Honey, every guy out there has a girl. This isn't marriage, it's payment." She yanked him down for a hard kiss, and the way her body pressed against him so firmly made all lucid thought fly out of his brain. She smelled strongly of sweet perfume. Her skin was warm, and her tongue was hot as it entered his mouth.

"Really, I can't. I can't," Kye said as strongly as he could. Having taken her by the hips to move her off of him, he was only vaguely aware he had yet to remove them.

"Listen," she said sternly, her doe eyes going narrow. "You're new here, so you don't quite understand what's at stake. I'm Max's when I ride up with the others from Vermont. If he's offered to share with you, that's a big deal," she said, prodding him in the chest. "Not only will Max be offended if you refuse, but he's also going to be pissed. Know what that means for me? I lose position. Do you know how hard I worked to get from blow jobs to arm candy? I'm not about to lose that because you want to take the moral high ground. If you think he's just going to be angry with me, you're wrong. He's going to be plenty pissed at you too. You'll be scraping gum off the bottom of the pool table the rest of your life if you don't play your cards right. So…" she said, taking a step back from him, "…be a good boy"— she continued as she unhooked her bra and let it fall to the floor— "…and just say 'thank you' after we're all done."

She closed the gap and started kissing him again. Her fingers moved quickly as they unbuttoned his shirt, and the heat of her bare chest against his made parts of him go rigid. Kye couldn't help the groan as she slid one hand down his pants and began rubbing him.

"That's it," she said in his ear before biting his earlobe. She took hold of his pants by the belt and turned to push him down onto the cot. Like a cat in heat, she straddled him and began yanking his pants down. Kye felt powerless against his fragile position in the gang and to his own hormones that were screaming for more of this eager woman. His resolve relented the moment his pants were off and her mouth found more than just his lips to devour. Laying back on the bed, every nerve in his body tingling, he didn't see his cell phone on the floor as it silently rang with a picture of Eliana lit up on the screen.

Eliana could feel the tears freezing on her face even as they fell. Despite her perfect GPA, flawless attendance record, and Harvard acceptance letter, Eliana had never felt more stupid in her life. Here she'd been sitting, waiting, fantasizing about that college apartment that was close to campus and the auto shop that Kye could work at. So, she sat. And waited. And dreamt. And of course, Kye didn't show—again.

"So stupid," she muttered angrily. Shoving her phone into her pocket, she descended the rope ladder and ducked out from under the willow tree. "You can pass advanced chemistry, but you can't take a hint." How many times had she tried calling him before the reality of his apathy set in? "Ten… you called him ten times…" she answered miserably as she walked across the park. The sound of her sniffles was lost, however, the roar of an approaching motorcycle shattered the quiet evening.

Eliana paused on the curb to let the biker pass, but to her dismay, it began slowing down. Her fear spiked when she saw the Screaming Demon logo. The bike stopped just before it reached her, and Eliana stumbled when she turned to run. Landing ass first in a snowdrift, she barely had time to scramble up before the man was right in front of her.

"Eli, hey wait!" Kye caught her by the arm as she was trying to stand, intending to help her up, but the shock of his voice coming from behind the bandana sent her sliding into the snow.

"Don't!" she snapped when he reached for her again. "Don't ever touch me again, Kye Driscoll!" She couldn't see it, but his face had paled.

"I know I'm late. I'm sorry I got hung up with…"

"What? You got hung up with what? Can't think of another lie!" She wasn't even attempting to stand anymore and in her rage, she began hurling snow at him. "You weren't at a college visit! Or have the Screaming Demons opened an academy now?" Kye looked somber when he pulled down the bandana, and he watched wordlessly as she stood. "So is this why you've been gone?" He nodded once. "Does this have anything to do with what happened to your leg?" Again, Kye nodded. Eliana scoffed and threw her hands in the air. "I don't even know who you are anymore."

"Come on, yes, you do!" he said, grabbing her hand and stopping her from storming off.

"The Kye Driscoll I spent all summer with never would have lied to me about getting shot!"

"How did you know?"

"Oh, come on, Kye, you don't need a degree in forensics to guess what a bullet wound looks like. I can't believe you got shot. What happened?" She had pulled her hand back and was holding it up to stop him. "No, wait. I don't want to know. I can't have anything to do with this. If I'm even associated I could lose my scholarship."

"That's not going to happen, I won't let it," Kye said adamantly.

"Yeah? How are you going to do that? Get shot and bleed on someone else's bathroom floor?"

"Ideally, I won't get shot again…"

"Are you kidding me? You're going to make jokes right now?" she asked and shoved his shoulders.

"I'm sorry, okay!" He took her by the arms and held her for fear she'd run away. "I'm sorry I lied. I'm sorry I put your scholarship at risk. I'm sorry I've been gone. You deserve better than this and trust me, it's not how I wanted to leave things."

"I'm still mad at you," Eliana said, crossing her arms but turning her body to face his. "Why did you have to join the Demons? Don't they sell, you know, drugs?"

"Among other things, but yeah, they do."

"Have you sold drugs?"

"Yes."

"Kye!"

"You wanted me to tell the truth, and that's what I'm doing. I've sold them, and I've made good money doing it too. I'm probably going to sell more. I'll sell as many as I need to put space between me and the streets."

"Is that what this is about?" Eliana asked, sniffling again. "Kye, you have other options than selling drugs and joining biker gangs."

"Like what? Harvard isn't exactly knocking on my door!" he defended.

"Don't you dare! I worked my ass off to get into that school. You don't get to trivialize it!" she screamed.

"Hey, I'm not," he said, dropping his voice and pulling her into his arms. "I know you worked hard and no one, not even me, gets to take that away from you." She finally stopped struggling and relaxed into his embrace. "I don't like every aspect of being a Demon. There are things I have to do that I don't like..." He forced the memory of red lips out of his mind. "I just need to get some money in my pocket and open up a few doors before I'm eighteen and kicked out."

"The Duncans are kicking you out?"

"They said I could stay on, but I'm not going to."

"Why? I don't understand," Eliana said as she tucked a section of hair behind one ear.

"You can't understand, Eli, you've never been in the foster system. It sucks," Kye said, kicking a piece of ice with his toe. "You're only as useful as your check every month, and you'd better not be more trouble than you're paid. Bounced from home to home, sleeping on a dirty mattress if they even have one. Watching kids get adopted, like Liam, while I'm constantly left behind... unwanted."

"You're not unwanted."

"Yes, I am," Kye snapped, his eyes growing watery. "I'm a seventeen-year-old with barely a passing GPA, and everything I own fits in a backpack. Who would want me?"

"I want you," Eliana said softly as she cupped his face. "You're my best friend. I want you."

"You're leaving too, Eli. We haven't talked about it, but you're going off to school..."

"You can come with," she said eagerly. "I have it all figured out. I have a room ready, and there's a couple of garages that said they'd interview you."

"I'm not going to get rich fixing cars."

"Who needs to be rich? We'd be together. Is that... is that not something you want?"

"Don't be ridiculous," he said, winding his hand behind her neck to turn her face up toward his. "I want to be with you more than anything. You're my reason for living." Her heart was pounding as his thumbs massaged her skin.

"Come with me then." Her eyes were rounded and looked pleading.

"We'll make a way to be together," he said gently. "Don't give up on me." Now Kye was pleading. Remnants of her earlier anger dissipated when he kissed her. Sliding her hands around his neck, she pulled him closer. The heat they generated blocked out the night air and, for a moment, their kiss blocked out everything in the cold world.

* * *

"COME ON, DAD," Eliana encouraged as she helped her father across the threshold. As if her evening needed any more drama, her kiss with Kye had been interrupted when her phone rang. Dino, the owner of Dino's Pub and Grub, was calling. Henry had run out of cash and was causing a scene when they wouldn't serve him anymore. Valiantly Kye had offered to go to the bar with her and help, but they both had concluded showing up in his Demon cut wouldn't deescalate the situation.

Eliana was still in disbelief that Kye had joined. The views on the club were mixed all over town. Some loved the business they brought to establishments, particularly the pool hall and strip club. The more domestic side of town couldn't stand them. Their bikes were loud, they drank too much, and their profit in the drug trade was untaxable.

Having never personally associated with them, Eliana was on the fence. On the one hand, she was never going to be able to support illegal behavior. Wasn't she going to school to defend the law? That wasn't entirely true. She knew there would be times she'd have to defend criminals and see that the justice system was upheld. On the other hand, she knew Kye, and she trusted him.

"Just leave me here," Henry groaned as he collapsed on the couch. Eliana brushed the hair out of her face and sighed. Taking the blanket off the back of the couch, she draped it over him. "That damn Dino thinks he's better than everyone..."

"Dad, you racked up a hundred-dollar tab that I had to pay. It's not Dino's fault you can't stop drinking."

"Don't you worry about the money, I'll make more money. I got some money coming in," he slurred as he dug in his pocket for his wallet. "I don't have it now, but I got some comin'."

"Right, when that comes in I'll put it with the money you were supposed to set aside for the gas bill. We're a month behind now."

"I got it coming, don't you worry..." Henry trailed off

as he lay back and closed his eyes. Eliana briefly stared at her drunk of a father and wondered if her lot in life was any better than Kye's. The agony of the foster system was beyond words but having to parent your parent was hell in itself too.

If only her mother hadn't died. How different would life be for her? Eliana had few but powerful memories of her life when she was little. Her daddy was her hero, and her mom was her best friend. The three of them used to go for long drives on the coast. She remembered singing and laughing and feeling the world was a bright and shining place. Now it felt cold, and it smelled of cheap whiskey.

Moving into the kitchen, Eliana opened the fridge for a late-night snack. Her thoughts drifted back to her raven-haired heartthrob. She let the memory of their kisses be her escape as she tried to drown out the sound of her snoring father. Sitting at the dining room table with her sandwich, she set her phone by the stack of mail. Deciding the bills could wait until morning, she grabbed her phone.

I'm scared… She hesitated before sending it.

Baby, what's scaring you? Her eyes welled up with tears at the pet name.

Drugs? Bullets? Motorcycles, you name it.

I have a helmet.

Will it deflect bullets?

I haven't tested it. Maybe? Despite the morbidity of their conversation, his text made her laugh. Kye could always make her laugh. Before she could type a response, his next message came through. I don't want you to be scared. What happened that night was a fluke.

Can you promise it won't happen again?

I can promise that I'll be careful. That's the best I can do for now. It didn't bring her much comfort, but she was grateful he was at least being honest with her now.

I wish we could just disappear. Go live on an island somewhere.

We'll discover our own island! Name it after its founder.

Naturally, I assume you mean yourself.

Duh. Kye Island sounds fantastic. Eliana Island sounds ridiculous. She had to cover her mouth she was laughing so loudly, and the last thing she wanted was her father ruining this happy moment. It amazed her how just a brief conversation with Kye could give her an escape from her life. Even sitting in front of a stack of unpaid bills one room over from her drunk father, she was already on that island with him.

It's all the 'L's. Too much of a mouthful.

I'd take a mouthful… By God, even in text he was making her flustered.

Kye Driscoll!

Yeah, baby?

I'm in love with you. She'd sent the text without even thinking, and there was a moment of sheer panic when she tried to hit 'delete' before it had gone through. Her hands were in a cold sweat while she waited for his reply.

I was hoping to say it first… I'm in love with you, Eliana Granville. Her giggle of delight mixed with the tears rolling down her face, she had to wipe her eyes with her sleeve just to see the screen.

Well if we waited for you to make the first move, it might take another nine months.

Touché. I won't make that mistake again.

Good. I'm trusting you.

I hope to never let you down.

Just don't break my heart, okay?

Never.

* * *

KYE FELT guilt sitting on his chest like a ton of bricks. He'd known he was never going to forgive himself for sleeping with Blondie, but did it have to be the same night he and Eliana exchanged 'I love you'? Tossing his phone onto his bed, he moved into the bathroom to take a shower. A very cold shower. He was going to scrub every inch of skin that Blondie had touched until he was positive nothing of her lingered. He knew when he joined the club that there would be things he'd have to do that he didn't like, but taking this method of payment hadn't even crossed his mind.

The showerhead might as well have pelted him with ice cubes the water was so cold. Why did it have to be Blondie? What would it feel like to have Eliana's lips on him that way? Lathering the soap, he scrubbed himself raw. His skin was red when he stepped out, and his teeth were rattling. He quickly dressed in sweatpants and was pulling his shirt on when he made it back to his bedroom where Stan and Carey were waiting.

"This can't be good…" he said under his breath. Stan was holding Kye's leather cut in one hand and Carey was sitting on the edge of the bed looking worried.

"Son?" Stan asked shortly as he extended the cut. Kye took it from him and hung it on the back of the chair. "That cut doesn't belong on you or in this house."

"Should I leave it outside?"

"Don't be nasty, Kye," Carey said sternly. "That gang is nothing but trouble. It's not the direction you need to be going in."

"We won't allow it, Kye. It's not an option," Stan agreed.

"I'm not giving up the club," Kye stated bluntly. "I'm sorry you don't like it, but I've decided."

"Not as long as you're living with us, Kye," Carey said with the first glint of tears in her eyes. "If any of your gang, or the drugs or violence make it back here, we could lose our license to foster."

"Your paychecks, you mean?" Kye asked defensively.

"Don't you talk to her like that," Stan snapped as he stood between them. "We have the right to set rules in this house, and you will obey them. Are you even working at Hal's garage, or was that a lie to cover where you've been? What about the college visit? Another lie?"

"Kye, you're headed down a slippery slope," Carey cautioned. "We've seen too many of our foster children get wrapped up in the wrong crowd. Your focus should be school and going to college. What about your friend, Eliana? She's the kind of person you need to be around. Do you two still talk?"

"Yeah, we still talk," Kye replied, and the guilt he felt over their last conversation sank in. No matter how cold he'd made the shower and how much soap he'd used, he couldn't get rid of the smell of Blondie's perfume.

"Well good," Stan said with an element of relief. "You know, she's got a bright future. She's sure to get into Harvard. You should focus on that relationship and not this Demons nonsense."

"Why don't you ask her to prom?"

"Prom?" Kye asked with a snort. "I'm not really one for school activities, Carey. I'm barely passing my classes as it is. Trust me, the school is just as ready to be rid of their foster charity case as I am to be done."

"Well, whose fault is that?" Stan asked with more severity in his voice. "Instead of studying or applying yourself, you're running around on a motorcycle with a gang of people who don't care about you. Not really."

"You don't know the first thing about them. I have friends. I matter to them. I'm someone important in the Demons!"

"That's what they tell you to get you hooked in. None of those guys care enough about you to act in your best interest. Are you on drugs?"

"What? No, I'm not on drugs. You know what? Forget it, I'm not your problem anymore," Kye said and grabbed his backpack from the hook on the door.

"Kye, don't do this," Carey pleaded as she watched him start to pack.

"Listen to me, son," Stan started and took Kye by the shoulders. "I know you want to feel like you belong to something, that you matter. But this club, this gang, is not the answer. It'll bring nothing but trouble to you."

"We hate to say it, Kye, but we can report gang activity to CPS," Carey threatened, but her voice was full of dread.

"You know what that means?" Stan asked. "They'll put you back in the detention center, son."

"Stop calling me that, I'm not your son!" Kye yelled and pushed his way past Stan to finish packing.

"You're not my son, but that doesn't mean I don't

care about you," Stan pointed out, and even his voice was shaking with restrained emotion. "We don't want to call CPS, but we will if we think it'll save your life."

"Go ahead, call them!" Kye challenged. "I called them six times when my last foster mother liked to put her cigarettes out on my back and arms. Took them three months to send someone. I turn eighteen in three days. Think they can make it that fast?"

"Kye, please," Carey pleaded as Kye moved for the doorway. He stood looking down at the round-faced woman whose eyes were red with tears. "Please," she asked one last time.

"It'll be for the best," Kye said solemnly as he grabbed his jacket from the chair. He ducked his head and gave Carey a small kiss on the cheek before pushing past her. She was still calling his name when he slammed the front door behind him.

7

The halls were littered with purple, green, and yellow posters promoting the upcoming Mardi Gras themed prom. The senior class, in particular, was bustling with excitement knowing that the end of the year was rapidly approaching. With March in full bloom, Spring fever was a way of life. The chill in the air hadn't quite left, but early buds of spring were forming on trees, and the sunny days were growing longer.

Eliana, in particular, felt her days dragging. Each agonizing morning she faced the same reality that her father was devoid of morality, and Kye was nowhere to be found. Sure, he'd text occasionally. Usually from different numbers. Burner phones more than likely. He'd barely been seen around the school and when he was, it was likely he avoided her altogether. Knowing that he was busy driving more business through the Screaming Demons, he'd made himself scarce.

Kye hadn't even been around for his birthday. Eliana had gone to the Duncans looking for Kye only to find he'd run away in the days before. Although disappointed, she wasn't necessarily surprised. Kye was on his own journey now, trying to discover himself and build a life he could be proud of. She couldn't judge him for it, but that didn't stop her from missing him. He'd called for her birthday, but since then, they'd barely spoken. That was near five weeks ago now.

Eliana had spent her eighteenth birthday holed up in her room blasting music. Her dad had picked up an extra shift at the lumberyard and had completely forgotten. Not that she could complain. In one of his more lucid moments he'd realized how far behind they were on bills and put in an extra effort to pay them off. Maybe it had been the afternoon he came home only to find the heat no longer turned on or that the lights weren't working, but he'd picked up extra shifts and stayed out of the bars long enough to get them caught up. He'd come home the night of her birthday with a bottle to celebrate. Without any patience to tolerate him, Eliana locked her door, turned her stereo up, and stuffed her nose into the first semester books she'd spent her savings to get.

"Who are you going to prom with?" Natalie, a girl in

her composition class, asked as the bell rang between periods. They'd just finished working on a project together, and Eliana had to admit, she'd enjoyed working with the short blonde-haired girl. They'd had a few outings for hot chocolate ever since and became fast friends. It was a nice relief to have someone to talk to.

"Oh, I don't think I'm going," Eliana said, trying to keep the sadness out of her voice. "I've got so much to do before I leave for college."

"I'm really happy for you, Eliana," Natalie said with a genuine smile. "I hope you'll come to prom, though. Some of us girls are going stag if you want to ride along! I mean, we're only teenagers once! You have to live to the fullest!"

"I'll think about it," Eliana agreed as she opened her locker to switch out her books for her next class. From behind her, Eliana could hear Missy's boisterous laugh. Since being elected prom queen, she'd been prancing around the school even more than usual. Not that Eliana cared. She had no desire for popularity, especially among social royalty like Missy Deacon. Eliana couldn't help feeling jealous. Why was she going to be robbed of enjoying prom because she didn't have a date? How much longer was she going to put her life on hold waiting for Kye to man up and date her properly? Was he waiting around for her? No, he was living his life without her!

Slamming her locker shut in determination, Eliana grabbed her cell phone and dialed the last number she had for Kye. It rang a few times before he answered.

"Eliana, I can't really talk right now."

"Kye Driscoll, if you hang up on me I'm never talking to you again!"

8

A man's ear-piercing scream of agony rattled the warehouse windows. Kye stood with sweat-soaked arms as he struck the man across the face again. His knuckles were sore, but at this rate, he wasn't about to relent. The bruised and bloody man hung his head, both of his arms tied behind his back as he was forcibly restrained on the chair.

"I told you, I don't know who's been skimming the inventory," the man repeated in a dry and scratchy voice.

"Six trucks in the last two months have gone missing after driving through here, Dean," Grier said from next to Kye. Max, who was standing in the corner of the room, nodded, and Kye punched the man in the face again. By this point, his left eye was so swollen Kye was certain there was permanent damage.

"Please," the man moaned in pain. "They all had full cargo when they left. I swear, Max, I swear it." Kye looked to Max who waved him over. The older man handed him a handkerchief that Kye used to wipe his swollen fingers.

"I don't think he knows anything, Max, we've been at this for six hours," Kye said in a low voice. From behind them, Grier took over the punishment and began striking blow after blow to the barely conscious man.

"Of course, he doesn't," Max agreed, and Kye looked at him incredulously. "Figured that out after the first hour."

"Then why turn him into ground beef?" Kye questioned. Max clamped a hand on his shoulder and offered him a cigarette which he took.

"You got a lot to learn, kid," Max began as he lit his Marlboro. "Between the last stop here in Vermont and the first drop off in Maine, we've lost near forty thousand in car parts. We can't keep escorting our runs across the border. We're drawing too much attention. Whoever is shorting our hauls knows we're looking for them. Dean and his fucked-up face are going to be an example to whoever has the nerve to mess with our products."

"Tensions are high with Vermont," Kye hinted. "There's the talk of splitting from Maine."

"You find whoever has been talking and you send

them the message, Vermont answers to me. Got it?"

"Yeah, Max, Grier and I will take care of it."

"Good boy," Max said, clapping him on the back. "I'm riding north with Riggs and Shon. We're going to find this asshole, and anyone working with him is dead."

"Won't let you down, boss," Kye promised, and Max gave him a fond smile. His role as the young prodigy was suiting him. While still working alongside Grier as muscle or backup, he noticed Max was trusting him with more jobs out of town without a more trusted rider like Hamilton. Max trusted him now and trust came with more green in his pocket. Kye had saved a few thousand now. The promise of more kept him hooked. For better or worse, he was a Screaming Demon now.

* * *

"Kye, you want in on this?" Grier asked as he brushed his long brown hair out of his face. In doing so, Grier smudged his forehead with blood. Before he could answer, he felt his phone ringing. Though he hadn't programmed her number into his most recent burner, he had her cell phone number memorized.

"Eliana, I can't really talk right now."

"Kye Driscoll, if you hang up on me I'm never talking to you again!" She sounded pissed. Not that he could blame her. Their relationship over the last month had felt more like a game of tug-of-war than anything.

"Okay, calm down. What's the matter? Are you alright?" He held his hand over the receiver as Dean cried out in pain, and Kye gave Grier a pleading look. The older man shrugged and paused in his ministrations to grab a drink from his bottle of water.

"No, I'm not," she said with anger still in her voice. "I'm sick of this. I'm not some fish on a hook, Kye. You've been tugging just hard enough to keep me on the line, and I don't like it."

"I know, but you told me to keep my distance when I'm out… you know, on business. I'm trying to respect your boundaries with my business team."

"That's just it, you're always out on business."

"Well, we've run into some issues with merchandise."

"I don't care," Eliana argued. "Listen, I'm going to prom."

"Prom?"

"Yeah, prom. P-R-O-M, prom! I'm sick and tired of missing out on the best moments of my life because of you or my dad or stupid Missy Deacon. I'm going to prom and that's that!"

"Yeah, no, I get it…" Kye could feel his head spinning. She was talking quickly, and the bleeding man in front of him was distracting. "Who are you going with?" Kye asked, feeling nervous. Even though she was anti-social,

Kye knew he wasn't the only boy with eyes in his head. Eliana was stunning and sweet. Maybe in the weeks he'd been gone, she'd found someone else…

"I'm going with you, ya idiot," she said in a calmer voice. "You're taking me to prom. I don't care if I have to go in a burlap sack. I'm going. You're taking me."

"Eli, I have my hands tied…" Dean looked up from his beaten haze to glare at Kye. The irony wasn't lost on them. "I may not be back in time."

"Then we're done, Kye," she said in a strong voice, but he could hear the emotion behind it. "I'm in love with you, and I want us to be together, but I'm done setting my hopes on men who disappoint me. If you can't do this one thing then…" she trailed off.

"Eli, I don't want to keep disappointing you. If you need me, I'll fight like hell to get back to you in time. I promise I'll do everything I can."

"Good."

"Eliana?"

"Yeah?" Her tone was back to the soft and melodious voice he dreamt of at night.

"I love you too." He could sense her smile through the phone, and Dean chose that moment to spit at him. Kye turned a glaring eye at him. "Baby, I need to go. I'll call you soon." He didn't wait for her reply before he hung up and drove his fist into the man's jaw. "Now, let's talk about the rumors of absconding…"

9

"I've gone to the only three shops we have in town, still nothing," Eliana said, disheartened. She and Natalie were finishing lunch, tossing the scraps from their trays into the garbage before exiting the cafeteria.

"Do you want to go into Portland this weekend? They have amazing boutiques. I can drive!" Natalie offered with the usual optimism in her voice.

"I wouldn't be able to afford anything from a boutique," Eliana replied as they stopped at Natalie's locker first, seeing that it was closer to the food court. "I nearly emptied my account to get my books for college. My scholarship pays for tuition the first year, but it doesn't cover books."

"Can your dad help? I thought you said he was

working more lately," Natalie asked as she finished grabbing her books, and they moved toward the adjoining hall toward Eliana's locker.

"My dad says he's bringing in more money, but I don't know where it goes. I had to bring him dinner three times at the lumberyard last week, so I know he's been there. I don't know. I'd hate to ask even. He gets so angry when I ask about money."

"Yeah..." Natalie said, unable to conjure any more suggestions. "What's going on over there?" she asked in a sudden change of subject. The hallway with Eliana's locker was crowded with students, but half of the hallway was dark, and students were gathered around something.

"Did someone start a fire?" Eliana asked incredulously as she saw the flickering lights of flames. "That's my locker!" she practically yelled. Knowing she'd left her college books inside, if her locker was on fire she'd never be able to afford more. "Oh my God..." she trailed off as she'd pushed her way through the crowd.

Surrounding her locker that was decorated with yellow Christmas lights were at least three dozen green, yellow, and purple-dyed roses with sparkling petals. A row of candles was placed directly in front of her locker, more rose petals littering the ground, and a large card with her name on it was taped to the front. Eliana felt her face grow hot as she noticed everyone was looking at her now.

"Well?" Natalie asked with ten times more excitement in her voice than Eliana would have imagined. "Open it!" The crowd of at least thirty students waited with bated breath as Eliana took the card in her trembling hands. Ripping open the white envelope, she saw a single page card inside that read 'OPEN ME'.

"I've forgotten my combination," Eliana said with a nervous laugh as she fumbled with the lock. She'd recognize that handwriting anywhere. After a few moments and several excited words of encouragement from the eager onlookers, Eliana was able to open her locker door. Another dozen white roses fell out, and dangling in the center of the locker was a tape recorder with a post-it note that said 'PLAY ME'.

Natalie, unable to contain herself, grabbed the tape recorder and hit play. Eliana couldn't even wrap her mind around the action enough to be angry. The excitement was palpable. Kye had done all of this? "Look," Natalie said, handing her the gift card taped to the back. Delilah's Boutique read the name on the front, and Eliana nearly passed out when she saw the amount it was credited with on the back.

"Eliana…" His voice sounded from the device that also had a loud rendition of 'When the Saints Go

Marching In' by Louis Armstrong playing in the background. "I don't have to tell you what an ass I've been not being around lately. If you could possibly forgive me, I would like you to do me the honor of attending prom with me." The music was still playing, and Eliana didn't quite know what to do when Natalie firmly tugged on her arm.

"What?" she asked, turning from her locker. With a small gasp escaping, she saw Kye standing behind her with a single red rose in hand. He looked better than ever, his crooked smile making her weak in the knees. "Kye," she whispered, and the first tear leaked out of the corner of her eye. As though they weren't the center of attention, he stepped toward her and wiped the tear off her face. "Kye, this is too much," she whispered, feeling entirely overwhelmed with elation.

"Well," he said gently, his hand still holding her face. "If you go in a potato sack, I'll wear a matching one." Bursting into laughter, she could only manage to shake her head no.

"Say yes already!" Natalie yelled, and the watching students chimed in.

"Yes, I'll go to prom with you!" Eliana yelled over the noise, and cheers were deafening. Kye picked her up in a firm hug, his face burying in her neck. His strong embrace putting all her broken pieces back together.

Loud whistles from the staff broke up the din as teachers hurried to find the cause of the noise and smell of smoke. The crowd of students quickly dissipated as everyone ran, fearing the threat of punishment.

"I have to go," Kye whispered with a mischievous smile as the assistant principal took hold of him by the elbow. Giving him a brief kiss on the cheek before he was pulled away, Eliana leaned back against her locker feeling that nothing in the world was going to stifle the butterflies in her stomach or tear the smile from her face. He'd come back for her and damn, he'd done it in style!

"I CAN'T DECIDE," Eliana admitted as she flopped onto the love seat in the dressing room of the boutique. Natalie, who'd followed through with her offer to drive them into the city, was phishing on a nearby rack for a dress for her new friend.

"I still can't believe he got you a gift card here," Natalie said, sitting on the couch next to her. "The cheapest dress is like five hundred dollars."

"Don't remind me. I get anxiety just looking at the price tags. I don't think I spend in one year what I'll likely end up spending today," Eliana said as she fiddled with the black and gold card from Kye. Unable to wait a minute longer, the two girls had left straight after school to the dress shop that was a nearly two-hour drive.

The place was incredible. It was the sort of private boutique only the ritziest of girls could shop. They'd been greeted at the door with flutes of sparkling cider and offered chocolate-covered strawberries. Having already bought her dress, Natalie was offering moral support as Eliana was subjected to the whims of her personal stylist.

"What about this one?" the stylist offered. Having scoured the mannequins for the finest dress, she was now presenting a dress made entirely of silver sequins.

"Wow," Natalie breathed as the gown was presented.

"I don't know," Eliana said hesitantly as she saw the thin straps and backless cut.

"Just try it on. How often are you going to get to do this?" Natalie had a point. Taking the dress from the stylist, she stepped behind the curtain and once again disrobed. She cursed under her breath as she heard her phone ring when she was halfway through removing her bra.

"Hello?" she asked without looking at the caller ID first.

"Hey, beautiful, what are you doing?" Kye asked from the other end of the phone.

"Currently I'm trying to unhook my bra," she said with a laugh as she switched the phone to her other ear.

"I could come over and help with that," he offered with a seductive lilt in his voice.

"Hmm, you could, but I'm not home. I went into the city. I'm trying on prom dresses thanks to a certain amazing guy I know."

"You went into town already?" he asked with a small laugh. "You weren't eager or anything, were you?"

"Kye, this goes without saying, but you have no idea how much that meant to me today. Despite the public humiliation, it…"—she trailed off for a moment as she slid the dress on over her head— "it meant the world to me that you came. And the whole production was so romantic."

"It's no less than you deserve," he said softly. "I wanted to make everything perfect for you. You were right, what you said on the phone the other day. Eliana, you've had to miss out on so many things. You've had to be an adult when you were just a kid. God knows your dad hasn't made things easier. The whole point of me doing what I'm doing— I just want to build a better life for you. For both of us. I want to make everything perfect for you."

"You're making me cry," she admitted as she dabbed at the corners of her eyes. "You mean so much to me."

"When are you coming back? I want to see you tonight."

"I don't know, probably late. It's still a couple of hours' drive back, and we're stopping for dinner before we leave. Natalie swears by this restaurant her aunt worked at."

"Damn, I really wanted to see you tonight. Getting pulled into the principal's office for my tardiness wasn't fun."

"Well gee, isn't the shoe on the other foot!" she teased. "Not so much fun when you're the one left behind while the other is out on an adventure."

"Very funny," he goaded. "Seriously, I'll wait up. I need to see you."

"Mmhmm."

"Have you at least found a dress yet? I was told Delilah's was the only place worth going." Eliana set the phone down for a moment to finish sliding up the zipper, and when she caught her own reflection, she felt a sensation overtake her that she'd never felt before.

With her hair pulled into a high ponytail, the long lines of her body were fully accentuated in the form-fitting gown. The silver sequins highlighted her porcelain complexion, and the way they sat over her waist and hips made her look more womanly than any of her stuffy sweaters ever had. Turning to peek over her shoulder, the plunging, backless dress turned her from

Plain Jane into a sexy, enticing lady. Eliana felt heat rise on her chest and face as she, for the first time, admired herself.

"Hello?"

"Oh!" she cried as she picked the phone up from the bench. "Sorry, zipper got stuck?"

"I was asking if you'd found a dress yet," Kyle repeated.

"Yeah..." she said, touching her chest where the heart-shaped neckline exposed just the right amount of cleavage. "I think I did..."

"What's it look like?"

"I want it to be a surprise. You, uh... you won't believe it."

"I'm sure you'll look amazing. Hurry home. I miss you."

"I will. Promise."

Eliana waved once as she stood at her front door. Natalie flashed the lights of her father's BMW before driving off. It was early in the predawn hours, and Eliana had accidentally let her phone die, so she hurried inside toting her gown in the dry-cleaning bag and a box with her matching shoes.

She was still reeling from her incredible day. Her

head felt light, and she walked on air as she moved inside. For the first time in her life, Eliana felt like a confident woman and not the scared girl she'd been most of her life. Since she could remember she'd felt desperate. Desperate for change, for an easier life, for a way out, a better grade, an escape of any kind. But today had taught her something. Kye had taught her something. Her new dress had taught her something.

Eliana was incredible. She was strong and passionate and borderline sensual in her own way. She felt so alive in her own skin she couldn't wait for prom and to show off her new skin. Maybe this was the confidence she needed to start her new life with Kye. She wouldn't walk into Harvard with her head hung low trying not to cause waves. No, Eliana Granville would walk into Harvard, recipient of a scholarship, with her head held high and a sway in her hips!

"Where have you been!" her father yelled. Eliana's heart plummeted as her father shot out of the dark kitchen to grab her by the arms. "You were gone, where were you?" The wild look in his eyes made the heat rush out of her body.

"I went dress shopping. For prom. I thought you'd be working late again, or I would have called before my phone died. What's wrong, Dad?" She'd seen her father in drunken fits before, but this bout of paranoia seemed off from his usual behavior.

"You can't go out like that. You can't just disappear. I need to know where you are. At all times! Do you understand me? Do you!" He was yelling and shaking her shoulders so violently she dropped her dress and shoes.

"You're hurting me," she said, struggling against him. When his grip tightened and she cried out, Henry stumbled backward and into the doorframe.

"I'm sorry," he said with large tears rolling down his face. "Liana, I'm sorry. I don't want you to get hurt. No one was ever supposed to get hurt."

"Daddy, what are you talking about? Who got hurt?" she questioned as she rubbed her sore shoulders. He was shaking his head as he turned and stumbled into the kitchen. Grabbing a bottle of brown liquid from the fridge, he stumbled toward her again, and Eliana couldn't help flinching when he reached for her. "Who got hurt?"

"No one," he said finally. "No one got hurt, and no one is going to get hurt, least of all you. You can't disappear like that. I need my Liana. You know I need you. I can't lose you too." Even though the smell of sweat and alcohol was rancid on him, Eliana allowed her father to hug her, and to her surprise, she felt him begin to sob.

"Dad, please don't cry," she pleaded as she rubbed him on the back. "I won't disappear again. I'll call next time, okay."

"No next time!" he snapped, and she jumped away from him as though he'd burnt her. Again, his eyes were wide, and he looked around rapidly before they settled back on her. "Best leave me, Liana," he relented as he began dragging himself up the stairs. She could still see his wide shoulders shaking with restrained tears as he vanished down the dark hallway.

Eliana waited until she heard his door close before retrieving her dress. Fortunately, the gown was protected in the garment bag, but she still pulled it out and examined it for damage after getting it to her bedroom. She felt anger at her father for robbing her of the delicious confidence she'd discovered that day. There was a need to retrieve it that welled within her.

With a fleeting whim, Eliana pulled a nightgown out of her bottom drawer. It was a satiny blue with a low neckline and sheer sleeves. Locking her bedroom door in case her father decided to stumble in, she stripped off her clothing and pulled the lacy material over her head. Having once belonged to her mother, it fit her nicely. Eliana resumed her position in front of the full-length mirror on the back of her door and appraised her appearance.

Without the guiding hand of a mother figure, she'd always been petrified of wearing something that was provocative in any way. She'd been almost fifteen and mortified when she'd had to buy her first bra. It had been a traumatizing experience walking into the secondhand store with what little cash she'd saved from babysitting and fumbled her way through the lingerie section. Had it not been for the matronly Mrs. Addlewood who worked the register, Eliana would have been lost to navigate the numbers and letters of cup size. Her fear of her own body had built a resentment toward it.

Now as she stared at her breasts as they hung heavy in the nightgown, she could see them in their beauty. They were round and full, with a light splatter of freckles on her collar area. The dip in her waist was high, making her hips look rounder, and she'd always been told she had long legs. Though never one for sports, Eliana had tried to remain a healthy weight. Not learning to drive yet offered her the chance to walk enough to keep any extra holiday pounds off.

It seemed scandalous to think it, but Eliana found that a generous amount of heat was rising in her belly as she moved around the room. She felt attractive. She felt sensual. It was a remarkable experience, but she felt immensely proud of herself for discovering this sensation all on her own. She was blooming.

As she brushed out her long hair, she found herself caressing her neck and wondering what it would feel like to have a man kiss her there. What would it feel like to have Kye kiss her there? Just the thought made her bite her lip. There was no denying the way he made her feel. The butterflies he gave her seemed amateur compared to her new-found eroticism.

Closing her eyes, Eliana leaned back on her bed, her hands still wandering and exploring her body, and she conjured images of her raven-haired love. How would Kye's hands feel if they touched her like this? She'd felt the roughness of his mechanic hands in only a few places, but she let her imagination explore the idea of how they'd touch her. How gentle would they be? What parts of his body would she discover first?

Her eyes shot open when she heard the rapping at her window. Feeling waves of embarrassment, she threw on her heavy bathrobe before tossing back the curtains and opening the window. The blast of cold air that hit her made her shiver, but not nearly as much as the sight of her previous fantasy standing in the cold.

"Good Lord, woman, I've been throwing rocks for twenty minutes," he whispered loudly. "Let me in!"

"Kye, I, uh, wait, no!" He was already rushing toward the back door, and Eliana felt panic overtake her. She didn't have time to redress, so instead, she tied her bathrobe on tighter before moving to the back door. The last thing she needed was her father bursting out of his room at the noise of Kye knocking.

"I nearly froze to death," Kye complained when she opened the door for him and they ducked into her bedroom. "What?" he asked, looking down at her after she closed and locked the door behind them. A strange expression had crossed her face, and his eyebrows raised as she looked him up and down with a slow and curious glance. "Eli?" he asked in a low tone when she pressed both her palms against his chest.

"You're cold," she noted in a voice filled with something he'd never heard from her before. Rising up on her toes, she pushed him against the door and pressed her mouth firmly, and daresay, hungrily over his.

Kye couldn't quite get his mind to catch up with what was happening. Logically he knew that gentle, soft-spoken, conservative Eliana wasn't pressing him against her bedroom door in a negligee with her tongue in his mouth, and yet the way his hands dug into her back to pull her closer would suggest otherwise. When he took a handful of her hair and tugged at the roots, her eager moan synchronized his senses to the realization 'yes, this is happening'.

"Eli," he croaked out when he had the lucidity to break the kiss, "what are you doing?"

"I'm kissing you," she replied, slightly out of breath. Before he could ask for elaboration, her lips were on his again, and the question flew from his mind. Taking another firm grip on the roots of her hair, he turned her around to reverse their positions, giving him a slight upper hand. The door rattled in its frame as he pressed her against it, and the way her back arched gave him the chance to wrap his free arm around her. God, she fit against him like the second half of a puzzle piece.

Without fully registering the thought, he couldn't believe he was finally holding her like this. His body craved her like any addict for a drug. Knowing she was relatively untouched, he'd sworn to himself never to push too far too fast, but with her panting in his arms, fingernails scratching the back of his neck, there was very little room for hesitation. Before he knew it, the back of his knees hit the edge of her bed, and they were toppling down. Rolling to partially lay on top of her, she raked a leg up his side, and he shed his coat to take hold of her smooth calf.

Eliana's hands, though shaking with uncertainty, snaked under the back of his shirt, and her nails dug into the muscles under his shoulder blades. The cold that had soaked into him from being outside so long was replaced with the heat of her body. His hands, not suffering from her shyness, had no problem dragging down the front of her nightdress and taking a handful of the soft fabric.

Her short breaths were hot in his ear when his lips moved from her mouth to her neck to her chest where her rosy pearls fit between his teeth. There was a rich smell to her, like chocolate and honey and that made him lightheaded. Eliana was moaning as he moved from one breast to the other, and she tugged deliciously at his hair. Her bare foot was stroking his outer thigh through his jeans, and his hips pressed more firmly against hers until his hip bone dug into hers. The sudden gasp she emitted alerted him that she'd felt his hardness tucked between them and like a bucket of water to a lit match, he flew off of her and stumbled into her dresser.

"What's wrong?" she asked, sitting up just as quickly. Her lips were bright red and swollen, and there were marks on her neck and chest where he'd been kissing her. "Kye?" she asked again with an almost hurt tone of voice as she pulled her top in place.

"Nothing," he said, shifting his weight at the uncomfortable pressure in his jeans. "Nothing is wrong, just going to stand… over here."

"Why?" she asked with confusion. She twisted so her legs dangled off the edge of the bed. The hem of her nightgown rode up, and her soft thighs were exposed. Kye turned his back to her and started fiddling with items on the top of her dresser. "Kye?"

"I'm just looking at your stuff," he said lamely as he mentally demanded that his body cool down before he exploded just from looking at her.

"Right now? I kinda thought we were in the middle of something…" He could still hear the passion in her voice. It dripped from her pouty lips like syrup. Oh, how he wanted to taste her dripping places. He could do it, you know. She was sending all the right signals. He could turn around, go to her, and strip that nightgown off… "Kye!"

"I just think we should slow down," he stated with a crack in his voice he hadn't heard since puberty. He was still examining a bottle of nail polish when he heard her stand and cross to him. Eliana's long arms wrapped around his middle, and her face buried in his back.

"I don't want to slow down," she admitted, her voice partially muffled in his shirt. He tensed as her hands ran down his chest toward his hips. Stopping her hands in place with his own, he turned around slowly and lifted her fingers to his lips and kissed them.

"I don't either, to be truthful," he likewise admitted.

"Then what's the problem?" she questioned with a hint of a giggle. Clearly, she expected them to resume because she stepped against him, her hips tucking into his again.

"Eli, don't," he said as strongly as he could. Taking hold of her hips and gently pushing her away, the hurt look returned to her eyes.

"You don't want…"

"I want everything!" he interrupted. "I want you. All of you. I want you naked on that bed underneath me until neither of us can walk straight." He laughed and ran a hand over his face as Eliana blushed furiously. "Not like this. Not a frantic fuck at two in the morning with your dad in the other room."

"It wouldn't be…"

"It would," he interrupted. "You have to trust me on this. It doesn't feel like it right now, but tomorrow it would, and I can't have that. You'd resent me for it, and I'd hate myself. We're better than that."

"Then… how?" she asked, and he allowed himself to pull her into his arms. He pressed his forehead against hers and she relaxed into him.

"We'll find the right time," he assured her as he rubbed her back. "We'll go slowly. Take our time. Without fear of someone walking in or either of us getting hurt. The next day we'll be more in love than ever and neither of us will have any regrets."

"That sounds perfect." She bit her lip, and Kye pressed his thumb into her chin until she released it. He kissed her more gently this time, and she sighed contentedly. "I don't want you to go tonight…"

"I won't," he agreed.

"Just hold me?" He nodded, and they stood for a moment with their arms wrapped around each other until their burning passions that had nearly incinerated them cooled into a warm affection neither of them had felt before.

Kye could tell she was getting sleepy by the way she rocked in place. He grinned as he bent and scooped her up. She giggled as he carried her to the bed and teasingly dropped her before jumping on top of her. She was shrieking into his chest while he tickled her sides and stomach.

Rolling onto his back, she leaned over him, her long hair creating a curtain. He cupped her face, and she gave him a long kiss. Eliana nestled her head on his chest, and he kicked his shoes off before she pulled her thick comforter over them. His thumb was rubbing slow circles on her shoulder when he felt her breathing change. Glancing down, he saw she had already begun to fall asleep.

Kye settled himself farther under the blankets, sure to keep Eliana as still as possible. She opened her eyes momentarily to look up at him, and they exchanged soft smiles. It felt perfect having her wrapped around him like this, and she felt the same about having him in her arms. Soon the room was filled with the sounds of their soft breathing, neither of them remembering a time when they slept so well.

WHEN ELIANA OPENED her eyes the next morning, she could still smell his cologne on her pillow even though Kye was nowhere to be seen. Sitting up, she looked around her room groggily and saw the Post-It note on her mirror. The wooden floor was cold under her feet, so after she retrieved it she dove back under the covers.

Good Morning. Left before your dad could wake up. I love you. A small arrow indicated she should turn it over. P.S. You snore. Eliana burst into laughter and set the note on her end table before stretching her arms overhead and flopping back onto her pillows. Closing her eyes, she conjured the memory of the night before. Though it hadn't ended the way she'd hoped, she couldn't deny how perfect it felt. She could feel his strong hands and how his rough callouses had felt on her legs, hair, and breasts. And his mouth? God, the things his tongue could do.

Covering her face with a pillow, she let out a shriek of embarrassed delight. She'd so willingly pulled him into her bed like a cat in heat. Did that make her 'easy'? Rolling over onto her stomach, she grabbed her phone and waited for it to power on.

No, she concluded. 'Easy' would mean any guy could come into my bed. I just want Kye. Thinking about her momentary embarrassment, how he'd now seen her topless, she was grateful he had stopped them. While she had, and still did, want to have sex with him, if they'd rushed into it the way they almost had, she definitely would have woken up with regrets. If possible, she felt she loved Kye even more now for the restraint and tenderness he'd treated her with.

I do not snore, she typed and sent off to him. She'd

only just gotten dressed when she heard his reply come in.

I was teasing. You don't snore. But you do drool…

Kye! I do not! She screamed while she typed and sent her reply. Unable to keep herself from laughing, she pulled on a pair of warm socks. I wish you hadn't left so early.

I'm sorry. I wish I could have stayed, but if your dad had caught us it would have ruined the moment.

I agree, she concluded. I agree with everything you said last night. Thanks for everything. I don't regret anything we did or anything we didn't do.

It wasn't easy. You know I want you, but I want you the right way.

I do too. And I want it to be soon.

Eager much? He teased.

Don't expect me to be embarrassed about that. I'm a woman who knows what I want, and I'm not afraid to go after it anymore.

One of the many reasons I love you. We'll make it soon. Very Soon.

Eliana was still smiling as she padded down the stairs and into the kitchen where she stopped dead in her tracks. Her father and her uncle Ron were standing over the dining room table with at least fifteen stacks of cash. They looked up at her when she entered the room.

"What. The. Hell?" Eliana asked, enunciating each

word pointedly. Stepping closer she saw each stack was sorted by denomination: fives, tens, twenties, fifties and the majority being hundred-dollar bills. "Dad?"

"Look, Liana, didn't I tell you I had money coming in?" he asked proudly as Uncle Ron went back to sorting from the pile in his hand.

"Dad, there's no way you came by this legally," Eliana observed and felt the heat drain from her body. She felt at any moment the front door would burst open and the cops would raid the place, and they'd all spend the rest of their lives in jail.

"Well, not exactly legal but not entirely illegal," Ron said, waving a hundred-dollar bill in the air.

"There must be thirty thousand dollars here!" Eliana exclaimed, wiping her sweaty hands on her pants. Could she wipe all her fingerprints off?

"So far, we have $67,235," Ron chimed in. Eliana glared at him, and he wordlessly went back to sorting the money.

"Explain," she demanded sternly with arms crossed and fixed her dad with a glare.

"Baby, listen," he said, guiding her away from the table. "Your uncle and I have been taking some… short-cuts at work."

"Shortcuts?"

"You know all those trips we take transporting lumber from up north to the mill and then down to

New Hampshire and Vermont?" he asked, and Eliana only nodded. "We get an advance for transportation. Once the timber is delivered, we keep the commission if it's delivered on time or under budget."

"There's no way you've commissioned $67,000 worth of timber!"

"Sixty-eight thousand!" Ron added, waving another bill. Henry motioned for him to be quiet.

"That's where the shortcuts come in. Do you remember Dean who used to work at the timber yard with me?"

"No."

"Oh… well he did, great guy, really," Henry said, stroking his beard. "Anyway, he secured us a freight box on the M and G for a small flat rate about two years ago when he moved south. We can transport whatever we need whenever we want."

"How does a shipping container on a freight train do any good?" Her head was spinning trying to put the pieces together.

"Because, Eli, that train cuts straight through the state and passes right by the timber yards we have to deliver to. Ron and I can cut nearly sixty hours off of our transportation time in one trip! Do you know what that commission adds up to in two years?"

"Sixty-eight thousand dollars?" she asked in a breathy tone as she looked back at the stacks of money.

"You see? It's perfect? Ron and I take the hardest contracts we can find, deliver under time, and keep the commission. Why do you think I've been gone so much? We are in hot demand!"

"We sure are!" Ron shouted and tossed the money he was holding into the air. It cascaded down like a millionaire's waterfall.

"Now, Liana, listen," Henry said, placing his hands on her shoulders and pulling her attention back. "We've got more to sort through, but after Ron and I split the money…"

"Fifty-fifty!"

"Right, fifty-fifty," Henry agreed with his brother, "I want you to take my half."

"What?" she cried. "Dad, no!"

"Don't argue with me," Henry scolded. "Ron and I have a good gig going on here. I can earn more. The house is paid for, and I'm a man of simple taste." Whiskey. "You've got school and Harvard and your whole life ahead of you! I want you to take the money and start a new life. A better one than I could ever give you here."

"Dad…" Tears were leaking from the corners of her eyes. She'd never seen so much sincerity from her dad in her entire life.

"Aw hell," Ron said with his hands on his hips. "If it's for your schooling, take ten percent of my cut. Lord knows I don't have any children to send off to school." Eliana was still standing in shock when Ron came around the table, and the two men hugged her. She couldn't force her mind to do the math and figure out what sixty percent of nearly seventy thousand dollars was at the moment, but she knew it was enough.

Enough for a new life for her and Kye.

10

Kye felt every muscle in his arms and back screaming as he lifted his chin above the bar for likely the hundredth time. Slowly lowering himself, sweat rolling down his face, he lifted himself back up with a grunt.

"Yo, whore!" Grier yelled as he threw a full soda can that hit him in the abdomen. The pain caused Kye to lose his grip and fall from the crossbar to the ground. Fortunately, he landed on his feet, but the spot where it had hit him turned red and would likely bruise.

"Asshole," Kye snapped and threw the can back at his friend who was seated on one of the couches near the pool tables. Grier ducked, and the can hit the wall where it exploded and fizzed all over the floor.

"I can't watch you do another pull-up," Grier said from his lounged position. Kye was walking over to him while wiping his face with his discarded t-shirt. "You've been doing nothing but exercise for three days; what are you pushing for, a modeling career?"

"Just trying to burn off some energy," Kye said as he dropped to the floor and began doing pushups.

"Need to get your dick sucked?" Grier asked as he shifted to rest his legs on Kye's bare back instead of the table where they'd been.

"I'm not interested in you like that," Kye stated as he goaded his friend.

"Breaking my heart, pretty boy, but I wasn't referring to me. Plenty of pussy to be had around here," Grier said and waved for one of the Wall Kats to join him. A redhead in fishnets moved eagerly to his side, and he pulled her onto his lap.

"No, thanks," Kye said, swatting Grier's feet off of his back as he stood and moved toward the punching bag.

"Want a joint?" Grier asked as the woman on his lap began kissing his neck.

"I'm good," Kye brushed off as he started practicing his punches at the red piece of equipment.

"Man, I don't get you," Grier said, standing from the couch, the redhead on his lap tumbling uselessly to the floor with a squeak. Grier stepped over her and joined his friend where he held the bag in place to assist Kye in his swings. "You don't partake of any of the spoils of war," Grier continued in an almost whine. "You don't get laid, you don't take a hit, and I've never even seen you with a beer in your hand. What are you, a boy scout?"

"I pocket my money, that's all the spoils I need," Kye stated before landing another one-two combo.

"Virgin," Grier insulted as he shoved the bag into him. Kye missed the block and took a hit to the chin then fell backward to the floor.

"How can I be a virgin when I've been fucking your mom every night this week?" Kye called after him. Grier stopped in his tracks and turned slowly to face Kye who was picking himself up off the mat, a cheeky grin on his face. Grier's nostrils were flaring with restrained anger. "Yeah, you'd better call home, man. You could be a big brother by now."

"You're dead," Grier snapped and hurled himself over the table to tackle Kye. The two boys rolled around on the ground exchanging punches and kicks, grabbing the attention of the other Demons. Starved for entertainment, the men and women in the clubhouse eagerly gathered to spectate.

The boisterous men began hooting and cheering on their choice of victor. Beers began cracking open as Grier took a hit to the jaw that filled his mouth with blood. Kye took an elbow to the sternum that knocked the wind out of him, and Grier took the opportunity to grab him in a headlock. Kye used his upper body strength to lift the other boy off the ground and slam him onto his back.

"We need help over here!" Everyone stopped in their tracks as the door to the clubhouse slammed open. Four of the senior Demons poured in, two of them carrying Max between them. Grier and Kye flew to their feet and hurried to help carry their leader over to one of the sofas.

"What happened?" Kye asked as he saw the blood pouring from Max's abdomen. He instinctively applied pressure hoping to stop the flow.

"We got ambushed just outside of town. Shon went down in the gunfire," Riggs answered. He was bleeding from somewhere under his helmet, and the red liquid was trickling down his forehead and nose.

"Who ambushed you?" Grier asked as he arrived with the medical kit from under the bar. He removed a thick roll of gauze and set to cleaning the wound.

"I don't know," Riggs said, shaking his head. One of the other members helped him take off his helmet and pressed a towel to his head.

"Another gang? The Rebel Riders?" a member asked. A sense of panic was setting in.

"No, they wore cuts, but they looked…" Riggs began but didn't finish. His face was pale.

"They were defectors," Wayne, the other senior rider

who had been carrying Max, answered. "They wore Demon cuts with brandished logos."

"Defectors?" Grier asked as he looked at Kye with concern. "I thought we squashed that rumor."

"Apparently not," Kye said quietly and with a shrug. His attention was drawn back to Max who began groaning as he awoke and tried to sit up. "Easy, Max, you've been shot," Kye said, placing a hand on his mentor's shoulder.

"No shit," Max answered, holding a hand to his side. "You," he barked at Grier, "go get Doctor Alan from the pharmacy on Hickory; he owes the club a favor. No one else, understood?" Grier nodded before scampering off at full speed. "Rest of you, piss off!" he yelled, and the others scattered. Max caught Kye by the arm to hold him in place as Riggs, Hamilton, Wayne and a rider named Duke all stayed.

"Who were they, Max?" Kye asked as he continued to try to keep Max still. Clearly, the man did not like laying in a position of vulnerability.

"I was right about it being an inside job," Max began, "whoever has been pilfering our merchandise was doing it to fund a chapter of defectors. They've built up a nest egg and now they're trying to weasel in on our routes. The boys and I were securing our warehouse when we got attacked. Not only did they know where the storage unit was, they knew we were coming."

"That's not possible," Kye replied, shaking his head. "That would mean the source of the defectors is…"

"In the New Hampshire chapter," Max finished. There was a moment of silence as the men all looked at each other in a mixture of shock and outrage. "With Shon dead, the list of people I trust begins and ends with you five," the older man admitted. "Until the dust clears and we figure out what the hell is going on, I don't want a single Demon riding solo. We travel armed and in pairs at the very least. Keep regular check-ins and no one leaves town, got it?"

"Yeah Max," Wayne replied with a nod.

"We should assign pairs," Kye suggested, and the others looked at him in suspicion. "If the source is in our chapter, then he probably recruited a partner if not more. Max, if you choose our riding partners then their leader is more likely to be caught."

"That seems a little extreme considering we don't know anything for sure," Duke began, but Max grunted his interruption.

"Kid has a point. The dam has sprung a leak, and I'll be rotting in my grave before I let some cock-sucking defector tear my gang apart out of greed. Once Grier gets back with the doctor, I want to see a list of all our chapter members."

"Some of them are out of town. We still have three distribution teams up north," Hamilton added.

"Then get on the phone and get them back here!" Max said through gritted teeth. Despite his paling complexion from the blood loss, his face was growing increasingly red with anger. "Duke, Wayne," he beckoned, "get a six-man team together and hit our warehouses. I want to know if we've lost anything besides a member today. Riggs, get yourself cleaned up and take the kid back to the storage unit. I want Shon's body brought back here before the cops find it."

"We're on it," Kye replied. "You going to be okay until we get back?" he asked, indicating the bullet wound that was still oozing.

"It'll take a hell of a lot more than a single gunshot wound to take me out of the game," Max retorted with a stern look on his face. "Don't let me down, son," he instructed, and Kye stood. "And if you catch sight of the sons-a-bitches who did this? Kill 'em."

IT WAS WELL past midnight when Kye and the others made it back to the clubhouse. They'd called ahead with the bad news. Three of the warehouses had been wiped clean that day. Knowing Max was going to be livid, the others sauntered off to the clubhouse to hide, while Kye went straight to Max's office where he noted the light was still on.

Quietly opening the door, Kye peered inside. He saw Max sitting on the edge of the oval-shaped table that occupied the center of the room. On the side, opposite where he was leaning, was a single, throne-like armchair covered in blue leather and black studs with the Screaming Demons logo branded on the back. On the nearest side were the four chairs that belonged to his 'horsemen' as he called them. Max, who was still shirt-less, a white bandage across his abdomen, waved Kye over when he saw him standing in the doorway.

"Kid," Max said in a surprisingly even tone. He was chewing on the blunt end of a cigar and a plume of smoke was rippling from the other. "Been a long day," he said and nursed a glass of brandy.

"You got the update?" Kye asked hesitantly. He didn't particularly want to incur Max's wrath, but neither did he want to be accused of withholding information. Since the deduction earlier that afternoon, everyone was walking on eggshells.

"I did," Max answered, still not looking up from the chair he was leaning in front of. "You're brave or stupid," Max said after he took another sip. "I haven't decided which one."

"Why is that?" Kye asked, closing the door behind him.

"Walking in here in person to tell me the news my

club is fucked," he replied and opened the decanter at his side to pour himself a second glass.

"I just thought you deserved to know," Kye admitted and accepted the second glass Max was offering him.

"I suppose that makes you respectable. None of the others bothered to stop by."

"I think they're all just a bit on edge. Everyone knows the hell we brought down on Vermont when we thought they were the moles. No one wants to be next," Kye said and rested his arm on the chair next to him.

"At least I still command some level of fear…"

"And respect," Kye interrupted. Max looked up at him, a small grin forming on his face. "These defectors got greedy, Max, we'll catch them and set everything right."

"Your youthful optimism is refreshing if not ignorant," Max said flatly and let out a long puff of smoke. "I've been around a long time, kid. I know fractures when I see them. I lost a loyal horseman today," Max said solemnly as he indicated the empty chair in front of him. As a prospect, having never been privy to the inner circle meetings, Kye could only assume it belonged to Shon.

"Who's going to take his place?" Kye inquired, hoping his question didn't sound insensitive.

"Hell if I know," Max admitted and stood upright with a slight wince as his wound stretched. "Can't trust my damn reflection at the moment let alone appoint a new horseman. They knew where we were today and didn't think twice about taking a shot at me. That says something."

"How so?"

"Think about it, kid," Max began as he moved around to the far side of the table and leaned his arms over the back of his throne, a cigar in one hand and brandy glass in the other. "If they were after just money, they would have tried to stay under the radar. You know, just skim the fat off the top and line their pockets. But lately, the thefts have been getting bigger. Noticeably bigger. They're leaving tags and now taking open shots. If I go down, the whole Demon structure caves in. They lose their cash flow. They're not just after money, they want chaos. Something changed. Things are personal now. I like your idea about pairing off, but not just to keep tabs on everyone."

"Why else?" Kye asked, already fearing the answer.

"Safety," Max finished. "Whoever took a shot at me isn't going to stop. They're going to take shots at any Demon they can find. And not just us. They're going to go after anyone they think is associated with us. We've found ourselves in the middle of a war, son. It's going to get ugly."

"You need another horseman, Max," Kye advised. "I know you think you can't trust anyone, but that's a good reason to pull more guys in. The closer you keep them, the better you can watch them. And you're going to need help doing it."

"I suppose you're suggesting yourself," Max concluded and gestured to the chair belonging to the late Shon. "Last guy who sat there died. You really want to bring that down on yourself? It's no small thing being appointed. You'll gain attention. And a target on your back."

"You said we all have targets. Mine will get a little bigger, but I can handle it. You need people close to you, Max, you know you can trust me." Max was silent for a long time. Kye stood patiently as the older man finished his drink and took a seat to enjoy the remainder of his cigar.

"I'll think about it, kid," Max stated. "You're right, I trust you, but I don't make this decision lightly. You find the man who started all of this, whoever has been stealing, you get a seat at the big table. Deal?" Max held out a free hand, and Kye wasted no time in taking it.

"Deal."

liana was pacing the living room with a clipboard in one hand, a pencil in her mouth, and two more secured in the bun on top of her head. She looked like a superintendent on a caffeine high the way she ticked off items on her self-made checklist.

"Items for donation..." she muttered as she pointed with the eraser end of her pencil to a stack of boxes near the door, "clothes to take to school..." she continued as she moved to aim her writing utensil at the suitcases on the couch. "Clothes to store"— her eyes searched the labyrinth of boxes before finding the ones she'd labeled on the coffee table— "check."

Running upstairs to gather a few more things, she paused to stare at her prom dress that was hanging from the closet doorframe. In all its shimmering glory, Eliana couldn't wait until she was dressed in it and dancing the night away with Kye. They were a week away from prom, and the days couldn't go fast enough.

Her stomach flipped as she ran her hands over the sequin material knowing it would be the last thing she wore before she gave up her virginity. Though he hadn't come right out and said it, Eliana knew Kye was thinking the same thing she was: the 'perfect moment' was at prom. Well, not at prom, but afterward. He was planning something special. It was evident in his voice when they'd spoken on the phone the night before last.

Something deep inside her began to hum and purr expectantly as she remembered their night together in her bed. How glorious would this next time be? Everything was falling in to place perfectly. They were one week from prom, three weeks from graduation and after their perfect night together, she'd tell Kye how she'd invested the second half of her savings to secure a larger apartment than a rented room. It was farther from campus but would easily accommodate two. Not just any two, but them. Kye and Eliana together in Massachusetts with a fresh life and no limitations.

Of course, she'd never get to the new place if she didn't finish getting her belongings packed. Though it was still a little early, Eliana wasn't going to leave anything to the last minute. Her room was already stored in boxes, minus the few essentials she'd need for the next month. Her storage space in the basement was cleaned out, and Eliana had been sure to pack the mementos of her mother's that she insisted on keeping.

Gathering a few more boxes to add to the collection, she glanced longingly at her prom dress one more time before carrying the load downstairs and placing them with the others. As she finished placing them amongst the hoard, she could hear her father's truck pulling into the driveway. She made a few quick notations on her sheet of paper on the clipboard before the front door opened.

"What's all this?" Henry called as he peered over a stack of boxes that blocked the doorway to the living room. He appeared surprisingly lucid despite the fact he'd been gone all day. Eliana was almost certain he'd gone on another bender since the night before.

"Just getting organized," Eliana called as she made her way through the constructed path to meet her dad. He was carrying a few bags of groceries, and she helped him set them in the kitchen where they had more room. "I have to send the last half of my deposit on to my apartment this week, but after that, I can start moving my things in. The landlord is going to make sure they get to my room so I should be able to ship most of my stuff."

"I see," Henry said softly as he sat at the table. She could tell there was a twinge of sadness in his voice.

"I didn't realize how much stuff I had," she continued, hoping to brighten the mood. "I've got almost ten boxes to donate to the thrift store. Mrs. Addlewood will be thrilled to replenish her stock. Clothing items were pretty scarce last time I was there."

"Were they?" Henry inquired, but his eyes were still fixated on his large hands. "Well you can take the truck," he said and fished in his pocket for the keys. They jingled momentarily as he extended them to her.

"Thanks, Daddy," she said sincerely as she reached for them. It wasn't often Eliana used the truck. More often than not, she'd have to take the keys and hide them so that her father wasn't tempted to drink and drive. Now as he offered them, she smiled with gratitude. When their hands met, he engulfed her petite hand in both of his large ones and pulled her close enough to kiss the back of her hand. "Are you okay?" she asked as she noted the large tears forming in his eyes.

"Don't you worry about me," he replied with a forced smile. "Your old man is just going to miss you, that's all. This house won't be the same without my little saint."

"I hate that nickname," Eliana said before she could stop herself. Although momentarily alarmed at her own boldness, she couldn't dispute the relief she felt once she'd finally said it.

"You do?" Henry asked in surprise. Eliana sighed and took the seat next to her dad. "Since when?"

"I don't know," she began, "always? I hate it when you

treat me like I'm perfect. I'm not perfect. I'm not a saint and…" she paused to muster some courage, "…I'm not Mom."

"You're so much like her, though."

"See, that's just it," she interrupted in annoyance. "I want to be able to hear that and feel proud. But every time you compare me to Mom it's because you're hurting, and you want to feel like she's not gone. I can't replace her, Dad. I'm still just a kid. I'm your daughter!" She could feel the start of a panicked set of tears welling up inside, and she tried to force them down.

"Oh," Henry supposed shortly. For lack of anything to say, he scratched at his beard and observed his daughter. He sat for a moment looking entirely perplexed before he brought himself to answer her. "I know that you're not your mother," he started with restraint. "I guess I just see so much of her in you. The way you smile reminds me of her. She was a kind woman, always saw the best in people, kind of like you."

"I don't always…" Eliana admitted.

"You know, neither did she," Henry said with a chuckle. "Why she married me, I'll never know. I think I bugged her into doing it. I only had to propose six times before she said yes."

"What?" Eliana asked in a shocked laugh. "You proposed six times? That must be some kind of record."

"I did," Henry confessed. "Of course, the first time I

proposed we were in second grade. I crafted a dandelion into a ring, you know, the way girls used to wear those in their hair?" he asked and reached out to tug a strand of hers playfully. "Took me all of recess to chase her down on the playground and ask her."

"She said no?"

"She said no. She said I had to color her a picture instead and of course, the only crayon I had that day was black. Your mother never cared for black. She'd dress like the rainbow anytime she had the chance."

"I remember that," Eliana said as a memory infiltrated her mind. "I remember when we'd go to church, she'd wear this bright orange hat with a yellow scarf around it. 'God made many colors, Liana, why do we wear only one at a time?' I can't believe I remember her telling me that..."

"She was a brilliant woman; she could glow in the dark she was so radiant," Henry continued, and the two fell into a momentary silence that passed with fondness. "Liana, when I call you a saint, I know it probably sounds unfair."

"Daddy..."

"No, let me say this," he interjected. "I never was much of a man without your mom. I've spent too much damn time in this town. I only left twice, and the things I saw overseas were things I hoped to never bring back with me..." he said, alluding to his short career in the military. Eliana knew only three things about his service in the Marines: he joined trying to be a hero, he was dishonorably discharged, and to never ask him about it. "I've done a lot of bad things in my life, and I guess the only way I felt better about doing them was because I told myself I was doing them for you and your mother."

"She's been gone a long time, Dad," Eliana said. She had a certain level of compassion for her father, but his helplessness triggered more pity in her than empathy.

"You won't remember this, but after you were born, your mom got sick. Really sick. Doctors couldn't figure out why she was still bleeding and how to stop it. Before surgery, she made me promise that no matter what, I'd do right by you. After she got better I thought, good, she's still around because God knows I don't know how to raise a daughter."

"I doubt any guy at your age would have."

"No, but a lot of guys would have done better. A lot better…" Henry reached across the table to take her hand again. "I let your mom down, Eliana," he said, using her full name for perhaps the first time in years. "I haven't done right by you. I'm sorry that things are this way. I'm sorry that I'm this way."

"Dad, we could use some of the money to get you into treatment," Eliana suggested. "It's not too late to turn things around. You know, I could help."

"No," Henry said solemnly, "you've done too much

for this old man already and, to be honest, I'd be too scared to get sober. Alcohol seems to be the only thing that keeps the demons away."

"Alcohol is a demon."

"I won't argue that, but it's a demon I know and have become comfortable with," Henry admitted.

"Well that makes one of us," Eliana said, pulling her hand away. "I need to get these groceries put away and take my boxes to the thrift store before it closes." As she stood, Henry grabbed her hand more forcefully this time.

"Liana, I'm sorry," he said quickly. "I know it's not the answer you want. I promise I will try to get clean and fix things between us. I don't want you to go off to college and never see you again. I just don't want you feeling like you have to take care of me anymore. You need to live your own life."

"I'll still visit sometimes," Eliana said, but even as the words left her mouth she nearly vomited. The idea of going to school and never returning was what had kept her strong for the last five years.

"I know you won't, Liana. There's nothing in this town for you except bad memories and a house that's barely standing," he said, gesturing to the walls around them. "But I just want to ask, if somehow, someway, I can sober up, maybe put on a pair of clean pants and shave," he said with a small laugh, "would it be ok if I came and visited sometime? Maybe at Christmas?" There was a childlike vulnerability in Henry's eyes that, had they not had the last thirteen years of baggage, might have moved her, but instead she found herself full of contempt.

"I don't know, Dad, you're going to have to give me some time to be there and get settled. I'll be really busy with homework and you know, I have a work-study program that's going to help me pay for school. I'll be working in the administration building, so I'll likely have to work holiday breaks…"

"I understand," Henry said, nodding and letting his hand drop from hers. "You've got a whole new life in store, and I won't stand in the way of that." A single tear dripped down his face, and Eliana felt her heart constrict painfully in her chest. Poor Henry Granville. Poor drunk and lonely Henry Granville.

"Maybe for New Year's, though," she suggested against her better judgment. Henry's face lit up in a smile. "We could go to Boston or something."

"Have a cup of clam chowder," he offered, and Eliana laughed.

"Sure, Daddy, we'll get a cup of red and white and see which one is better." Henry stood and wrapped her into a large hug. Eliana hugged him back with all the hopes that maybe, one day, their pretend fantasy of eating chowder on the bay would actually come true.

Though she wished it, she knew better than to expect it.

"You'd best get going," Henry suggested as they broke the hug. "I'll put the groceries away, and you get those boxes moving. Only a few weeks left of school, I imagine you'll want to have your stuff ready by then."

"That's the idea," she agreed. "The sooner I get my stuff sent, the sooner I can start my summer job and put some money aside."

"Speaking of which," Henry said as though he'd remembered something. "Before you go to the thrift shop, I want you to go to the bank, put this money into your account." He handed her a paper money order with more zeros on it than she'd expected.

"Dad…"

"You need to be quick about it too," he insisted, "some shady things going on around town. Been seeing a lot of motorcycles from those Screaming Demons and a fair amount of cop cars. Not sure what the raucous is, but I don't want you wrapped up in any of it."

"I'm not going to get put on an FBI watch list for depositing this much money, am I?" she asked, only partially joking.

"I don't know about the FBI, but I took out the money order myself. I told the director of the bank that I'd sold my stock in the lumberyard, and they didn't ask any questions."

"Thank you, Daddy," she said and stood on her tiptoes to kiss her father on the cheek. He wrapped an arm around her in a quick hug before she pocketed the money order and left the room to pack up the boxes.

Henry heaved a heavy sigh. As he watched Eliana finish packing up the truck and pull out of the driveway, he couldn't help but think of that sweet, pigtailed little girl who used to dance around the living room playing a toy trumpet and singing 'When the Saints Go Marching In' as loudly as she could. That little girl was long gone now. Long gone and almost out of reach for poor Henry Granville.

"When is this prison sentence going to end?" Grier asked as he, Kye, and three others moseyed into the twenty-four-hour diner on Main street. Their bikes were parked under the overhang outside as the early spring rain poured.

"Hardly a prison sentence," Kye noted as the five of them slid into a booth near the register. "At least we're allowed out of the clubhouse."

"In groups like a fucking field trip," Grier grumbled, and they ordered a round of milkshakes and burgers from the older woman working the late shift. Even Kye couldn't deny how restless he was getting. They'd spent the better part of three weeks since the incident with Max working internal investigations. Prospects weren't allowed out without being in groups of three or more and even the patched members were on restrictions.

Feeling like they were under the watchful eye of their babysitter, this evening's being Wayne, they all felt more than a little on edge.

"Move," Wayne barked as he shoved Grier out of the booth.

"Where are you going?" Grier asked harshly as he rubbed his shoulder where he'd landed hard on the red and white tile floor.

"To take a piss," Wayne snapped back, "wanna hold my dick for me?"

"Hell no, I'm not your sister!" Wayne flipped him off as he moved toward the bathroom, and Kye helped Grier to his feet. "That guy is an asshole," Grier stated as he slid back into the vinyl booth.

"He's stressed like the rest of us," Nathan, one of the other prospects said. "Think one of us should go check on him?"

"There are sides of Wayne I don't want to see. You go check if you're that worried," Kye suggested. Nathan and his brother, Zeke, stood and followed after their bald-headed senior.

"Something weird about that," Kye thought out loud and watched the two boys disappear into the bathroom.

"Think it's a circle-jerk?" Grier asked as he dove into the fries that had been delivered to the table.

"You're a dumbass," Kye stated and leaned a little

closer to Grier. "When have you known Wayne to ride out with prospects?"

"Never," Grier answered with a mouthful.

"So… you don't think it's weird he asked us?"

"What are you implying?"

"I don't know, man," Kye said, leaning back as he noticed the three guys heading back their way. "Just keep your eyes open. You're the only one I trust right now."

"See, that means a lot to me," Grier chided with a teasing smile. Although he was kidding, Grier admittedly felt the same way toward his friend. The two were more like brothers than friends, especially after all they'd been through the last few months of prospecting. "What's that all about?" Grier asked in a sudden change of subject. Kye looked over his shoulder where Grier was pointing and saw Wayne, Nathan, and Zeke surrounding someone near the front register. Their hoots and taunts gave the impression they'd found someone to taunt.

"Probably just messing with one of the locals. You know how they get when they're bored."

"Yeah, she's kinda cute, though," Grier commented. Kye turned completely in his seat to get a better view, and he felt his heart drop when he saw the brunette trying to push her way through them.

"Eli…"

* * *

"I HATE YOU!" Eliana screamed with all the rage that was pent up inside of her. Henry was fumbling about, a pitcher of water in one hand and a roll of paper towels in the other.

"Don't yell!" Henry complained as his bloodshot eyes twitched frantically. Eliana grabbed the paper towels from him and desperately tried to dry off the ruined books and papers on the counter. The air was still thick with smoke, and overhead the circular smoke detector was blaring.

"Don't touch anything!" Eliana yelled and used her shoe to smash the smoke detector off the ceiling. It fell to the floor, and she stomped on it several times until it stopped beeping. As silence fell in the room, she turned to survey the damage. The entire kitchen counter was charred, bits of plastic pieces were melted, and the stack of college books along with her carefully mapped out plans for Harvard were singed black.

"It was an accident, Liana," Henry said, still lamely holding the water pitcher. "I was trying to cook dinner a-an-and…"

"And what?" she snapped before picking up the empty bottle of whiskey from the counter. "Had a little drink? Dad, my books are ruined! Do you know how much those cost?"

"I'll buy you more…"

"I don't want any more money from you! In fact, I don't want anything from you ever again! Don't talk to me, don't look at me, and I swear to God if you so much as touch any of my belongings before I move out in two weeks, I will set the rest of the house on fire myself!"

"Don't say that…"

"I'm done with you!" Eliana hurled the bottle against the wall, the glass shattering and spraying around the room like needles. Grabbing her raincoat, she stormed from the house, slamming the door behind her.

HAVING SPENT the entire day holed up in the library finishing her senior project that was due before graduation, Eliana could sense something was wrong even as she walked up the driveway. It was late March and the snow had turned to rain, but even through the thick drops, she could see the smoke billowing out of the kitchen window. Racing inside, she saw the metal pot on the stove had completely melted, and the heat had caused the dishtowels to catch fire. Sitting so near to the counter where she'd been studying her textbooks over breakfast that morning, three of the five freshman books were completely incinerated, and the other two were still burning.

She'd screamed for her father, who was passed out with his head resting on the dining table. He'd only come-to after she'd put the flames out. In his entirely unhelpful manner, Henry had grabbed one of the pitchers of water that held several of her roses and poured it over the counter where her papers were. What damage hadn't been caused by fire and smoke, the water had completed.

Eliana was fuming with rage even as her feet carried her into town. She now understood why Kye had left the Duncans' house early. Once the prospect of freedom was near, it was hard to find any reason to stay. Now that Eliana had a small fortune in her bank account and graduation was less than a month away, she was at the end of her rope. Thirteen years of tolerating her father's bullshit was enough. No more.

Her temper was momentarily interrupted by the growl in her stomach. Without realizing it, she had gone the whole day without eating. Taking a sharp left, Eliana ducked into Mauve's Diner. With her hood from her sweatshirt pulled over her head to shield her from the rain, she hadn't seen the motorcycles parked out front.

"Just one please," Eliana said to the older woman who was clearly working by herself that evening. Not that it made a difference, the place was a ghost town. With the recent increase in crime, the streets were rarely crowded despite the warming weather. As Eliana followed the older woman toward the crescent-shaped counter, she found her path blocked by two boys who couldn't have been much older than her.

"Where you going, sweetheart?" one of them asked in a suggestive tone. Eliana glanced up at him and then to the other boy, who she could only assume to be his twin brother based on their similarities in appearance, and kept walking.

"Woah, woah, not so fast!" the second boy said, standing in front of her. "Let's see that pretty face." He pulled the hood to her sweatshirt back, and she swatted at his hand.

"Feisty!" the first boy taunted and held her upper arms from behind.

"Come on, why don't you let us buy you a milk-shake?" the second and taller of the boys said as he stood directly in front of her. "If you're good, I'll let you lick the whipped cream."

"Get off me!" Eliana snapped and shoved him with all her strength. The boy tumbled backward and into the chair behind him causing a loud commotion.

"What's this?" an older, bald-headed man asked as he rounded the corner from the bathroom. It was then Eliana noticed the Screaming Demon logo on his leather vest. She felt the heat drain from her face. The grip on her upper arms had tightened and she squirmed, trying to free herself.

"Found a playmate, Wayne," the boy behind her said and Wayne, the bald man, shamelessly looked her up and down.

"Doesn't look like much," he observed and took a hold of her chin.

"Don't touch me," Eliana protested and made to slap him away, but he caught her hand. A short game of tug-of-war began as she tried to pull her hand back, but his strong grip didn't relent.

"Then again, this could be fun," Wayne said to the boy behind her. His face had turned into a mixture of amusement and something predatory that caused a trickle of panic to crawl up Eliana's spine.

"I'll call the police!" the small voice of the older woman behind the counter called over the raucous.

"No, you won't," Wayne observed without so much as looking up at her. He tugged Eliana toward him, and she felt utterly repulsed as he wrapped his arms around her. "Come here, sweet thing," he said into her ear.

"No!" she screamed and kneed him in the groin. He doubled over, and Eliana turned to run when she was caught by one of the twins. She screamed again, and the others laughed.

"Boys, boys, boys," a loud voice called over the commotion. Eliana tore herself free from the shorter twin and smacked into another leather-clad vest. This boy was definitely her age and similar height. He had curly blond hair and dark green eyes that were full of mirth and determination. "You've got no way with the ladies," he said, slinging an arm around Eliana's shoulders. She was about to push him away when he spun her around to face the direction he'd come and to her astonishment, she saw Kye sitting in a booth looking stoically at her.

"Ky.."

"Why don't we order you some food," the blond boy interrupted and walked her to the counter across from the booth. Eliana was too stunned to say anything as they walked past Kye. He didn't so much as stand up when they did. "Go on now, get whatever you like." Eliana looked up at the boy who still had his arm around her shoulder, she realized now was more protectively than anything, and shook her head.

"I'm not hungry anymore," she protested and slid from his grasp.

"They won't bother you anymore," he said quietly, and Eliana looked over his shoulder to see the three harassers from before were still laughing with each other but making their way out the front with cigarettes in their hands.

"Why are you helping me, aren't you with them?" she asked, still baffled why Kye was sitting there in silence.

"Technically…" he said, trailing off, but his charming smile had returned, "but as your boyfriend is my best friend, I've got divided loyalty. Go order something, and I'll walk you out," he instructed. With an urging nod, Eliana walked back to the counter and the older woman, who looked near fainting, took her food order.

"You have no idea how much I owe you," Kye said in a lowered voice to Grier, who was still standing near the edge of his booth.

"You just sit there and keep quiet," Grier suggested. "If any of those chumps find out she's your girl, it'll be bad news for both of you."

"You're sure about that? I hate just sitting here. She's going to hate me…"

"At least she'll be alive," Grier interrupted in a serious tone. "Everyone knows you have a bid for the fourth chair, and it's rubbing a lot of the other guys wrong. Especially the guys who've been around longer than you, like Zeke and Nathan."

"They'd really try to get to me through her?" Kye asked, and Grier gave him a look that informed him just how stupid that question was. "Can you get her out of here?"

"Sure, man," Grier agreed and clapped his friend on the shoulder before making his way back to Eliana. She was sitting at the counter, still shaking, when the older waitress handed over the paper sack with her food. Clearly wracked with guilt, Eliana didn't even have to pay. "I'll walk you out," Grier offered, and Eliana stared longingly over at Kye who could only send her an apologetic look.

"Why is he just sitting there?" she asked in confusion and bitterness. Wasn't Kye supposed to be the one coming to her rescue? Running interference between her and his gang?

"I'll explain, just…" He trailed off as the bell above the door rang, and the three guys came back in. "Act like you like me." Throwing his arm around her shoulder again, he guided her toward the door.

"Where are you going?" Wayne asked as he stopped them in the doorway. Eliana felt a wave of fear overtake her, and Grier tucked her closer.

"Party girl owes me a favor for buying her dinner," he said suggestively. "Won't be long." Wayne looked from Grier down to Eliana who did her best to look placid.

"You've got ten minutes," Wayne relented. "This cherry looks tight, I doubt you'll last five."

"I'll do my best," Grier said, chuckling and hurrying out the door with Eliana still tucked under his arm. When they were outside into the night and around the corner of the diner, Eliana pulled away from him and huffed loudly. "You could say thanks," Grier called, and she stopped in her tracks.

"Thanks? Those assholes are your friends! They were going to rape me!"

"I doubt that," Grier said, pulling a cigarette from his

cut and lighting it. "They'd have copped a few feels and gotten you all riled up, but rape? Doubt it."

"Gee, I feel so much better," she said sarcastically.

"You should, you have no idea how bad that could have gotten."

"You said they weren't going to rape me…"

"Wouldn't stop them from beating the shit out of you and your boyfriend," Grier offered. Eliana looked confused again, and he walked toward her. "Aren't you wondering why Kye just sat there?"

"Of course…"

"He's making something of himself in the Demons. He's rising in the ranks, and fast. He's got a target on his back, and there's a lot of guys who would love to tear him to pieces. They're going after him and anyone he cares about. Like you."

"Why? I don't have anything to do with your gang."

"Like it or not, if you're with Kye, you have a lot to do with us. It's not personal—it's politics."

"So Kye asked you to step in?" she asked softly as understanding overcame her, though it did little to settle her nerves. Grier nodded and handed her a cigarette. Without fully understanding why she took it from him, she inhaled her first drag of nicotine. Letting it out with a cough, Grier laughed and took it back.

"You are cherry, aren't you?" he asked with amusement, and she glared at him. "Don't worry, I like my women sluttier than you."

"Thanks?"

"You're welcome," he tossed back, and Eliana smiled softly. "Is he going to be okay?"

"Kye?"

"Yeah."

"I don't know," Grier admitted and the two exchanged looks and sighed simultaneously. "Let's get you home."

13

"Holy shit," Grier laughed as Kye walked into the main room of the clubhouse. Though members were crowded in small pockets, most turned to throw catcalls and whistles at Kye as he made his way through the room. His black hair was styled into a classy slick-back look, and instead of his usual cotton shirt and jeans, he wore a black suit jacket over a silver satin dress shirt complete with a metallic black bowtie and matching black slacks. His leather shoes were shined to perfection, and he'd bought himself a new watch with a reflective face.

"Thank you, thank you!" Kye called to the onlookers who didn't relent in their amused jeers.

"You look like one of those douches who plays piano in a fancy department store," Grier goaded as he joined him in walking toward the front of the building.

"Coincidentally, I applied for a job as one of those douches who plays piano at a department store," Kye teased.

"Can't believe you're bothering with prom, how lame is that?" Grier asked, but there was an element of envy to his voice.

"It's completely lame, but if it makes Eli happy, then it's what I'm going to do," Kye replied and struggled to find a way to put his helmet on without messing up his hair.

"So she wasn't mad about the other night?"

"I don't think mad exactly explains it," Kye confessed as he straddled his bike that he'd recently cleaned to an immaculate sheen. "She knows there are things I can't tell her, most of them she doesn't want to be involved in anyway…"

"It's unavoidable," Grier added, and the cautionary tone of his voice wasn't lost on him. "If you were smart, you'd initiate her as a Wall Mouse and get it over with."

"So another guy can drool all over her? You're crazy," Kye scoffed. "Besides, Eli has a future planned that definitely doesn't involve the Demons."

"Then why are you trying so hard with her?" Grier asked with evident confusion. Kye sighed as he started up his bike.

"Because I love her and no matter what, I'm going to find a way to be with her."

"You're so whipped," Grier joked, and Kye only smiled because it was true. Grier watched Kye drive off, the envy he felt for his friend welling up inside him before he felt a firm hand on his shoulder. Turning, he saw Wayne staring him down with six others standing behind him. He swallowed hard. This was going to hurt.

* * *

IT WAS impossible for Eliana not to feel entirely radiant. She'd spent all day getting ready, and with the help of Natalie's curling iron, she looked damned near flawless from the top of her curly-haired head to the tips of her home-manicured toes.

Usually opting for the natural look, Eliana allowed herself to explore the adventure of cosmetics and high-lighted her light brown eyes with black liner and bronze shadow. Her crimson red lips couldn't stop smiling as she slipped on her slightly heeled blue shoes. They clicked against the hardwood as she hurried downstairs.

"Wow, Liana," Henry said from the doorway. Her jaw set more firmly. She was still angry with her father, and it showed. "You look beautiful," he complimented.

"You shaved," Eliana observed when he stooped to kiss her on the cheek. Henry ran a hand over his now smooth face and shrugged.

"I needed it," he admitted, and Eliana could only nod.

"I saw the moving truck," he said softly. The small box truck was still sitting in the driveway nearly half full of her things for college.

"The landlord is letting me move my things in early since I paid up for the year. I figured it would be easier to take a couple of trips than to try to ship anything. I still have a few weeks of school, so I'll be back before Monday," Eliana explained. Now it was Henry's turn to nod. They fell into silence for a brief moment before the roar of Kye's approaching bike disrupted it. "I have to go," she said hurriedly and made her way out the front door.

"Wow," Kye breathed and swallowed hard as he watched Eliana race out her front door toward him. Every curve of her delicate body was enhanced by the flowing gown that sparkled in the setting sun. Her long hair was alive with curls that bounced as she walked toward him, and her apple-colored lips looked delicious as they beamed in a smile.

"Not so bad yourself," she admired as he dismounted and took her into his arms. She kissed him firmly on the mouth and giggled when she left a trace of lipstick on his lips. Using her thumb, she wiped it off, and Kye's eyes burned into hers. He was about to claim her in another kiss when he saw her dad standing just outside the front door. Kye gently turned her around to face her dad. "What?" she asked with vexation, and Kye's hand on her bare back made her rethink her tone. "What is it, Dad?"

"I just thought…" He trailed off for a moment, and that was when she saw the old digital camera dangling from his wrist.

"Here," Kye said, coming to his girlfriend's father's aid. "Let's get one of you and your dad," he offered and took the camera from Henry. They exchanged momentary glances, and Kye felt a prickling of familiarity that disturbed him.

"Let's hurry please," Eliana said, standing next to her dad. Kye snapped a few shots, unable to take his eyes off of her. In turn, Henry took a few pictures of Eliana and Kye, but her annoyance was clear.

"I'll let you go," he said quietly, and Eliana kissed him briefly on the cheek. "Have fun," he encouraged, and she smiled softly.

"Thanks, Daddy." Henry somberly moved inside with one spiteful glance at the moving truck. "You're going to make me ride that?" Eliana asked with a laugh as Kye led her to his motorcycle, which she had to admit to herself was gorgeous.

"Mmhmm," Kye replied, looking down at her with a grin as he draped his coat around her shoulders and began buckling the spare helmet on.

"I'll probably fall off and die," she admitted as she

slipped her arms through the sleeves. His cologne was still fresh on the lapel, and the aroma made her swoon.

"I don't know about that," he began as he slid his arms around her, his fingers pressing into the lowest point of her back. "You might like it," he said, barely above a whisper before he kissed her again. Eliana practically melted into his firm chest as she pressed into him. The mid-spring air was warm, but they both shivered simultaneously. "We should go," he said after breaking the kiss. Eliana bit her lip, and Kye groaned dramatically, which in turn made her laugh.

"If you insist," she teased, and he helped her sit onto the back of the bike. The slit in her dress opened as she did, and Kye couldn't help but imagine how glorious it would be to slide his hand up her inner thigh… "Is this alright?" she asked innocently, and Kye nodded, not trusting his voice. He quickly put his helmet on and took his position on the front of the bike.

"Hold on to me," he instructed as he kicked the bike to life. Silently following his instruction, Eliana pressed herself against his back, her hands wrapping around his abdomen. She didn't see the way his eyes closed in bliss at the feel of her, and he didn't see the way her knees gripped the seat tighter as the vibration of the bike between her legs made her squirm. What they did feel was the utter contentment of finally be together.

* * *

KYE COULDN'T HELP his smile as he watched Eliana twirling and laughing with her friend on the dance floor. He was seated at one of the tables on the perimeter of the wood floor of the school gymnasium, nursing the obligatory glass of punch while he watched her. They'd had a relatively uneventful meal before the DJ began blasting music, and Eliana had been pulled away by her boisterous friend Natalie.

Watching her dance unashamedly, jumping up and down, and racing to grab the Mardi Gras beads the hosts at the stage occasionally threw brought joy to Kye he couldn't fully explain. Eliana was blooming. She was no longer the shy girl in the background. There was confidence she now inhibited that made her all the more alluring.

As the music finally turned to something slower, Kye knew he couldn't keep his hands from her any longer and was quick to her side. "Excuse us," he said politely to Natalie as he wrapped a strong arm around Eliana's waist and pulled her against him. Natalie was smiling and giving Eliana two thumbs up as she walked away.

"Hi," Eliana said breathlessly as she laced her fingers together behind Kye's neck. He raised both eyebrows as he looked down at her, and her deep breaths caused her chest to rub against his.

"Hi," he responded and led her confidently in their first dance together. The soft jazzy music and the dim lighting created the perfect romantic moment, and when she gingerly rested her head on his shoulder, Kye couldn't think of anywhere else he'd rather be. The intoxicating scent of honey filled him to capacity, and he couldn't help the way his grip tightened around her. He only realized how tightly he was holding her when she gasped. "Sorry," he quickly apologized, and she pulled away enough to smile at him.

"I don't mind," she admitted, and the look she gave him through her long lashes made his pulse rise. He ran a hand through her soft hair before taking her by the back of the head and kissing her. A teacher walked past and cleared their throat loudly, and Eliana laughed when they were forced to part. "Killjoy," Eliana whispered to Kye as their history teacher sauntered away.

The music faded and before the next song began, the principal took the stage. "It's time to announce this year's senior class prom king and queen!" she called, and all eyes turned.

"Think I'll win?" Kye asked sarcastically, and Eliana laughed loudly. She took one of his hands in both of hers and pulled him off the dance floor. "Where are we going?" he asked, bemused when she didn't stop at their table, but instead continued out of the side entrance to the gym that led to the courtyard.

"I don't want to listen to Missy's 'you really like me' speech," Eliana said, casting a look over her shoulder that reminded Kye intensely of the half-lidded, sultry way she'd looked at him the night he'd slept in her room. He felt his mouth go dry when she stopped under a tree and leaned against the trunk. "Come here," she beckoned as she reached a hand for him. He diligently obeyed and took her by the waist.

"Have I told you how beautiful you are?" he asked as his fingers found their way to the bare skin of her back. The plunging cut made his head spin as he traced the indent of her spine.

"I don't mind hearing it," she confessed and savored the way he made her shiver and burn at the same time.

"Are you cold?" he asked as she pulled him closer by the collar of his shirt. Her curls danced over her shoulder as she shook her head. Her breath tickled his face as he ducked his head to kiss her. Part of him felt a great sense of pride at the moan she emitted, and another part of him felt personally challenged to see exactly how many of those heart-thumping moans he could elicit from her.

Eliana's fingernails were raking over the back of his neck, his hot mouth moving hungrily over hers. She pressed her hips so forcibly against his that Kye had to recover his balance by lifting her onto the edge of the brick wall. Without shame, her legs opened, and he occupied the space between them. The fabric of his slacks felt smooth on her bare inner thigh as she drew her knee along his outer leg.

Her teeth grazed his bottom lip, and she hesitantly nipped at it. When Kye inhaled sharply, she took the encouragement and pulled his lip deeper into her mouth. The feel of her tongue caused such a strong reaction in him that Kye felt every ounce of resolve melting away. He was hard, and she was eager.

"I want you," she breathed against his mouth when his hands took her thighs, and his thumbs were dangerously close to her heat. Kye kissed her passionately, but when she leaned against him he pulled back.

"Eli," he said and swallowed the lump in his throat. He was about to speak again when she cut him off.

"I'm visiting my new apartment in Cambridge this weekend," she said quickly. "I've got the moving truck nearly packed. I was going to leave in the morning, but… I want you to come with me.

"All weekend?" he asked with a raised eyebrow. She was biting her lip again, but this time it was clearly out of nerves. Kye slowly reached into his front pocket and removed a rectangular key card. Eliana stared at it blankly for a moment before he handed it to her. On the opposite side, she saw the hotel logo printed on it. Her eyes darted up to his. "We don't have to use this…"

"I want to," she said, taking his hand and pulling him

down for another kiss. "I want to more than anything." She was smiling from ear to ear, and the euphoria of anticipation between them only grew. "I thought maybe you didn't want me that way…"

"Christ, are you joking?" he asked with a laugh. "I want you every way imaginable," he admitted, and Eliana felt heat rush to her face. "I wanted it to be special, though. For both of us."

"I don't think it's going to get more special than tonight," she agreed. "Everything has been perfect. You're perfect."

"I'm not perfect," Kye said, shaking his head and taking her face in his hands. "But I am entirely in love with you." He kissed her forehead, and she smiled. Holding up the keycard she met his eyes.

"Then… what are we waiting for?"

"Yo-you want to go? Right now?"

"Right. Now," she confirmed by enunciating every word. Kye kissed her quickly before grabbing her hand and leading her toward the gymnasium to grab their coats and his keys. Eliana couldn't help the giggle as they practically ran.

"Miss Granville!" The two stopped in their tracks just shy of the door as the teacher who had interrupted their kiss on the dance floor was hurrying toward them. Preparing for the impending lecture, both Kye and Eliana groaned.

"Yes, Mrs. Watson?"

"You need to come with me," the tall woman said with an exasperated look. "It's your father."

"My father? What about him?"

"He's here."

14

The two-lane road that led out of Pine Hill cut through the woods bordering Maine and New Hampshire. The night was in full swing, and the dark clouds overhead obscured any light that the moon or stars could offer. When the front tires of the moving truck rolled over the yellow speed bump indicating they'd just exited town, Eliana let the tears flow. The salty drops mixed with her liquid eyeliner causing it to run and sting her eyes painfully. No longer caring how she looked, she used the back of her hand to wipe them free so as not to crash while she drove.

It was a tempting thought, though. To crash. To drive right off the edge of the bridge and into oblivion. However, as fate would have it, there was barely a twenty-foot drop to the shallow river, and she doubted the height was enough to do anything more than warrant a tow truck and Band-Aids. Gripping the wheel tighter, she steeled her gaze and focused on the road ahead.

After all, that was the only option now. There was nothing for her left back in town. Nothing. And no one. Not anymore.

* * *

"LIANA, LIANA, GET OVER HERE!" her father called as she and Kye, along with the teacher who'd located them, raced back inside the gym. Her father was stumbling through the crowd of students who were gawking with patronizing amusement. Their pointing and laughing only added to Eliana's mortification.

"Dad, what the hell?" she asked as she pulled him to a corner of the room. Eliana didn't know whether to take comfort in the fact that the principal and two other teachers were making their way over.

"We have to leave, now. It all went wrong. We have to go." He grabbed Eliana's arm and started pulling her from the room. They made it into the adjoining hallway that was lined with lockers before she ripped her arm away. Kye was faithfully at her side, but he looked just as perplexed as she did.

"I'm not going anywhere with you. You're drunk, Dad!" she snapped, and Henry looked ready to explode.

"You don't get it! They're going to kill me and probably you. We have to go! Leave town, forever!"

"Who's going to kill you?" Kye asked, sounding like the only voice of reason at the moment.

"You!" Henry said and shoved Kye into the metal lockers.

"Dad!" Eliana shrieked and stood between the two of them.

"I know what you are, you little shit!" Henry cried and pushed Eliana out of the way to grab Kye by the collar and slam him into the wall again. "You're a damn Demon, and you're the ones who set me up!"

"I didn't do anything," Kye argued and pushed Henry off of him.

"Mr. Granville!" the principal shrieked. "We've called the police. I suggest you get yourself home before they arrive."

"I'll take him," Eliana said reluctantly to the three authority figures who were staring them down. She grabbed her dad's arm and pulled him from the building out the front entrance before any more commotion was caused. "Give me your keys," she demanded as she yanked them from the pocket of his overalls. Henry didn't utter a single protest as he climbed into the passenger seat of his truck. "I can't believe this is happening," Eliana said to Kye, and she began to cry. He cupped her face and kissed her forehead.

"This doesn't change anything," he told her softly. "Get him home. I'll meet you there, then we're out of here. For good." Eliana nodded wordlessly and kissed Kye before he helped her into the driver's seat. He held her hand for an extra moment, pressing his lips briefly to her knuckles, before he closed the door and watched her drive off toward her house.

He had only just retrieved his suit jacket and Eliana's handbag and made it back to his bike when he saw the lone rider speeding toward him. "What the hell?" he asked when the bike nearly collided with his. Recognizing Grier anywhere, Kye called out his name when he toppled off his bike and onto the wet grass. "Grier, what happened?" he questioned and knelt next to his friend who hadn't even bothered putting on his helmet.

"We're fucked," Grier replied with difficulty. His face was a mess of cuts and bruises that were still swelling. His lip was split in two places, and his left eye was bulging from the broken blood vessels.

"Who did this?"

"Wayne, it was Wayne and Dean. They've been working together."

"Dean? From Vermont?"

"They've been the ones defecting. Dean has had it out for you since our 'interrogation' a few months ago. Now that he's gotten numbers in the Maine chapter, he's hauled ass to get here. He's in town, and he's looking for you."

"So let him find me. I'll drag his bloody ass right into Max's office and serve him on a platter," Kye said, helping his friend to his feet.

"No, you don't get it," Grier said, clutching his ribs that were likely broken. "It's bigger than that. Wayne and Dean have been smuggling supplies on the train line using stored box trucks from the lumberyard. They've got enough cash to recruit members. They're wiping out all of their ties to cover their tracks before they overhaul our club. We're not talking six or seven members—we're talking dozens. You have to get to the clubhouse. All of the loyal Demons are making a stand."

"Wait…" Kye said, forcing his mind to slow down. "What box trucks were they using?" Kye asked, feeling afraid of the answers.

"What does that matter?"

"Answer me!"

"I don't know, lots of trucks. Probably ones from the steel and lumberyards. They had some sort of commission scam going with— where are you going!" Grier yelled as Kye was already racing toward his motorcycle.

"You idiot!" Kye hollered. "Eliana's dad runs the lumberyard. He was in on that scam! That means Dean is after him."

"Fuck, man," Grier said, placing a hand on his

shoulder to halt him. "I had to give them something," Grier confessed, and his right eye conveyed his terror. "I told Wayne about you and Eliana. I had to give them something. They were hellbent on preventing you from getting in with Max. They were going to kill me. I didn't know what to do."

"Then they're going to kill Eli too," Kye breathed and revved the engine. Grier pulled the pistol out of the back of his jeans and handed it to Kye.

"I'm going to grab the others, we're right behind you." Kye didn't wait to hear the end of the sentence as he was already speeding off.

* * *

"YOU'RE NOT MAKING ANY SENSE," Eliana complained as her dad fumbled through his words. He was babbling as he hurried throughout the house, throwing his belongings around. Some of them made it into the back of the moving truck that he'd pulled onto the lawn, but most of them were littering the grass and the staircase. Eliana was standing in the doorway, still in her gown, praying that Kye would arrive to rescue her.

"They set me up!" Henry said for the five hundredth time.

"Dad, stop!" she yelled, and he paused on the bottom step. "Explain."

"I felt so bad," he began with large tears rolling down his face. "I ruined your books. I wanted to buy you more. I was going to do one more run, but the train doesn't travel this weekend, so I thought I could drive and I'd be fine…" Eliana was listening, but she sighed audibly in relief when she saw Kye pulling into the driveway. He was racing toward her as her dad continued to explain. "I'd driven the road once before, and I knew I could do it as long as I didn't stop. Last time I stopped I got caught. I lost the merchandise and had to shoot my way out…"

"What?" Eliana and Kye asked at the same time. Henry was sweating profusely, and his hands were shaking. Eliana couldn't tell if he was drunk or craving one. "The last time I lost a truck, they were going to kill me, but I paid them off. Some punk took the truck when I stopped at the checkpoint."

"Kye…" Eliana said, grabbing his arm.

"When?" Kye asked, his jaw clenched. Henry was quiet as his mind raced, trying to remember the date.

"After Christmas, before the New Year…" Kye shrugged Eliana's hand off his arm and launched himself at Henry.

"Kye!" she screamed as she watched helplessly as the two men brawled in the foyer. "Dad, stop, please!" she pleaded.

"You shot me! You almost killed me!" Kye hollered,

and his fist collided with Henry's jaw with a sickening crunch. Henry, though not as fit, still carried his own weight and threw the smaller man off. Kye crashed into the window next to the front door, and glass shattered everywhere.

"That was you?" Henry asked as he struggled to pick himself up. "I will kill you!" he threatened, but before he could reach Kye, Eliana stepped between them, both of her hands on her dad's chest to keep him at bay.

"If you kill him, you're going through me first," Eliana declared with more ferocity than she ever thought herself capable of. She felt Kye stand behind her as Henry's wild eyes glared down at his only child.

"He's a Demon, they're the ones who set me up," Henry protested. "They caught me with the truck. They think I was the one stealing everything."

"Weren't you?" she asked accusatorily.

"No, I was just transporting. I never touched a thing! I got paid to move it across the border, that's it! I'd send lumber down on the train, and they'd send the truck back with whatever stuff they wanted. I didn't even unload the shit!"

"It's worse than that, Eli," Kye said, drawing her eyes back to his. "The Demons are facing a split. I'm on the wrong end of a guy who's out for blood, and they know you're my girl. The Demons want to kill your dad for stealing, and Wayne and his men want to kill your dad so they don't get pinned for crimes. They're gunning for me for blowing the operation and you for being with me. You have to get out of town. Fast."

"I told you!" Henry chimed in.

"I'm not leaving you," Eliana argued as she turned to fully face Kye. He placed a hand on her face.

"Don't touch her," Henry yelled and shoved Kye's shoulder. In turn, Kye swung at him again, and the two started exchanging blows once again before everyone froze when the roar of motorcycles could be heard in the distance.

"We don't have time for this!" Kye shouted. "Eli, get that moving truck out of here. If the house is empty, maybe they'll move on. Your dad and I will be right behind you," Kye said, and Henry tossed her the keys to the truck. The impending arrival of either Demon or Defector put the fear of God into all three of them, and without another word of protest, they were all off.

Eliana led the way toward the edge of town in the moving truck packed with mostly her belongings. Henry followed close behind, and Kye took the rear on his motorcycle.

The front tires of the box truck made a grinding sound as they slammed into the horizontal speed bump that marked the end of Pine Hill. She had just wiped the tears from her face when several popping noises broke through the air.

Two red motorcycles rode in front of them from behind the line of trees. Even from her distance, Eliana could see the red spark of muzzle fire from their guns. She watched helplessly as the front tires of her father's truck were shot out, and he swerved several times before crashing into the ditch on the left side of the road. Eliana slammed the brakes before she rear-ended him, and she couldn't help her scream of fear as more gunfire echoed and the windshield was cracked to her right as a bullet ricocheted.

"Eli!" Kye hollered and jumped off his bike. He raced to her side of the truck and threw the door open. "Come on!" he said, pulling her out, and they ran to the silver truck that was in the ditch. Using the sidearm Grier gave him, Kye shot at the two bikers who were spraying them with gunfire. He fired off three rounds; two hit their mark, and bodies dropped to the ground.

Behind them they could hear more bikes rumbling, the headlights were drawing near, and soon more gunfire would ensue. Knowing the two dead riders were Wayne's men, they'd likely called in reinforcements to gun down Henry's truck before he could skip town.

"Daddy!" Eliana wept as her father spilled from the driver's seat. His forehead was bleeding, but he was otherwise unharmed. Kye and Eliana both took an arm and propped him up against the side of the vehicle.

"They know it's you, Henry," Kye said firmly, and the

older man nodded his understanding. The bikes were crossing the bridge now. "They're not going to stop until they catch you."

"Leave me," Henry suggested. "Take my daughter and go…"

"I'm sorry," Kye said, standing. His attention wasn't on Henry, though. His eyes were mournfully looking at Eliana. "You need to go."

"What?" she asked, feeling paralyzed with fear. "Kye, no!"

"Henry, I'm in love with your daughter," Kye said as a single tear fell from his eye and rolled down his cheek. "I need you to take her as far away from Pine Hill as you can. Don't tell anyone where you are and don't come back. No matter who wins this war, you're both in danger."

"Kye…"

"I'll take your truck and lead them away. If you love her, you'll take her. Now!" Henry didn't hesitate as he grabbed Eliana by the arm and pulled her toward the still running moving truck.

"Kye! No!" Eliana shouted. She pulled away from Henry and threw herself into Kye's arms. He caught her and let her kiss him. Though he stood stoically, internally his heart was breaking. The bikes were drawing near. "I love you," she wailed as Henry grabbed her around the waist and carried her flailing body. "Kye!

Kye! Don't leave me!" Henry forced her into the cab of the truck before climbing in after her.

"I love you too," Kye whispered as more tears fell. He caught one last glimpse of her pounding on the passenger window as they drove past. Sliding into Henry's smoking, silver truck, Kye managed to turn the vehicle around to face Wayne's men. The ride leading them was clearly dead. "Come and get me, you son of a bitch…" he muttered and pressed the gas pedal to the floor.

15

"Shots!"

Eliana was laying on the poolside lawn chair when two of her friends, Lyndsey and Kate, came racing over in their bikinis carrying trays of brightly colored liquor in plastic shot glasses.

"Here," Kate said, handing one to Eliana before sitting next to her. The music was blaring as the sun began setting, and nearly thirty college students were mingling around the sorority house. "You earned it, girl," Kate said, and they slammed their glasses back.

"Yes, I do," Eliana declared boldly and with a slight slur.

"Come here, come here!" Lyndsey beckoned as she jumped on the chair behind her. She pulled Eliana and Kate into the frame of her cell phone as she took the selfie. "This is going on Instagram!"

"Don't tag me!" Eliana ordered, and Lyndsey rolled her eyes.

"I know, I know, you're afraid of identity theft!" Lyndsey teased, and Eliana swatted her hand away before adjusting her own two-piece swimsuit.

"Cyberstalking is a real thing," Eliana muttered, and Kate handed her another glass. "Mmm, not too much," she protested. "I still have to finish writing my speech."

"Girl, stop," Kate said, lounging back on her lawn chair. "You've rewritten the damned speech seventeen times. Do you know how I know that?"

"How?" Eliana asked, feigning indifference.

"Because we've heard it seventeen times!" Lyndsey chimed, and both girls laughed.

"Fine, I'll read it to someone else next time!"

"No, you won't, you skinny bitch; you love us," Lyndsey teased, and Eliana threw an ice cube from her drink at her. Lyndsey shrieked and grabbed Eliana by the foot and dragged her into the pool with a large splash. They both surfaced laughing and splashing each other.

"God, I'm going to miss this," Kate sighed from the edge of the pool. "Why can't you go to medical school with Lyndsey and me?"

"Because," Eliana replied as she wiped the water out of her eyes, "someone has to bail your asses out when you get sued for malpractice!"

"Did she just say…?" Kate began, but Lyndsey, who was likewise scoffing, was already tackling her friend again. Kate jumped into the pool, and the three commenced in a splash fight that drew several onlookers in to join the fun. With final exams finished and ink drying on their diplomas, there wasn't a soon-to-be Harvard graduate who wasn't ready to cut loose!

* * *

"THERE YOU ARE!" Lyndsey said as she stumbled through the door to Eliana and Kate's shared bedroom on the top floor of the sorority house. She was carrying a bottle of tequila and three cups. The party downstairs was raging, and the house shook from the blasting music. Lyndsey kicked the door shut behind her, and stumbled over to Eliana's bed where they were lounging. "It's so loud," she complained and flopped her head onto the pillow.

"Why do you think we're hiding up here?" Kate asked rhetorically.

"How sad does this room look?" Lyndsey stated as she observed the boxes her two best friends were storing their lives in. "I can't believe we graduate in two days. I don't know how I would have survived these last four years without you two."

"You mean, who would you have cheated off of?"

Kate asked, and all three of them burst into laughter. "What is all this stuff anyway?" Kate slid off the bed and began rummaging through the perfectly alphabetized boxes at the end of Eliana's bed.

"Just some old stuff," she said nonchalantly. Her head was still spinning from the several shots she'd taken, and she was only vaguely aware of the items Kate was discovering.

"I've seen this," Lyndsey said, grabbing a white leather-bound notebook Kate was holding. Standing on Kate's bed, she flipped it open and pretended to read. "Dear Diary, today I had passionate, wild sex with Alan Meinke from Poly-Psy…"

"No!" Eliana screeched, and Kate tackled her as Lyndsey continued her dramatic monologue.

"The only thing bigger than his fabulous brain and intrusive ego is his massive, engorged donkey schlong!" Eliana was screaming, Kate was laughing, and Lyndsey stumbled off the bed and crashed hard onto the floor before curling into a fit of laughter.

"You did not just say 'donkey schlong'!" Kate said with tears of mirth in her eyes. Eliana managed to push her off and rolled onto the floor where she grabbed the journal.

"It does not say that," Eliana protested, and Lyndsey groaned as she tried to stand. Clearly, there would be a bruise on her side from the hard impact, but in her drunken state, it seemed to be the funniest thing ever.

"Liana likes her some big, hairy, donkey schlongs!"

"Just add bestiality to her resume for law school."

"Having sex with Alan Meinke would be bestiality; he's a pig," Eliana reasoned and tucked the book back into the box.

"Mmm, but he's so hot," Lyndsey cooed, sitting on the edge of the bed next to Kate. "What's that?" she asked suddenly and picked up a photograph from the floor that had fallen out of her diary. "Ho-ly shit, girl!" Eliana paled and reached for the picture when she realized what it was only to have Lyndsey pull it away.

"Let me see!" Kate hollered, and Lyndsey handed it over. "Wow, look at you, sexy-mamma! Why haven't I seen you in something sparkly and backless?"

"Stop, guys, give it back," Eliana pleaded but relented her effort to grab the photograph for fear it may rip. "That picture is a million years old from stupid senior prom. I totally forgot I had it."

"So, spill already! Who's the tall, dark-haired sex in a suit? He's a lot more than a random prom date."

"Liana, he's gorgeous, like… ten of Alan Meinke!" Kate added, and Eliana shoved her way between them to lounge on her bed.

"His name was… I mean, is Kye Driscoll. We met the summer before senior year."

"And?" the two girls asked together.

"And what? W-w-we went to prom together, that's all…" she answered vaguely.

"You are going to need to learn to lie better before law school, sweet cheeks," Kate teased, and Eliana was able to snag the picture from her. Looking down at it, she felt her heart flutter, and the sensation frustrated her. After all these years— four years two weeks and five days to be exact, just the sight of his picture brought all those memories and feelings back.

It had taken almost a year for her father and her to find somewhere to settle after they'd fled Pine Hill. After declaring her intended apartment to be unsafe because Kye knew the address, she'd had to cancel her lease. Bouncing from motel, hotel, and eventually an apartment two towns over from Harvard that required three bus trips to get to classes, they'd unpacked the few boxes they'd managed to escape with. Henry had gotten the pictures developed from their last night in town. Prom night. This particular one was of her and Kye standing under the tree in her front yard.

He looked incredible in his black and silver suit with his hair pulled back and his blue eyes beaming. Eliana was turned slightly and pressed into his side. Her eyes weren't on the camera as she was looking up at him with a brilliant smile. Just seeing herself so happy made her smile softly.

"He was my first love," Eliana admitted, and Kate and Lyndsey squeaked simultaneously. "But that's all history now," she said decidedly and set the picture on her end table.

"What happened? I mean, you haven't really mentioned him," Lyndsey asked.

"It's a long story."

"Well, good news is— we're not going anywhere!" Pulling the cork out of the Patron bottle, Lyndsey poured three more shots and passed them around.

"Oh, why not," Eliana relented and cringed as she downed hers.

"Spill!" Kate demanded.

"Pine Hill was kind of a brutal town," Eliana began, already feeling the effects of the alcohol. "All quaint and charm on the surface, but there was a lot of crime. Smuggling. Drugs. Stolen car rings."

"Ooh, this sounds like the plot to a mystery novel!" Lyndsey elbowed Kate in the ribs to shut her up.

"I didn't know it at the time, but my dad got involved with a lot of it. He ran the lumberyard and would illegally export lumber on the train line, fudge the numbers to look like he'd been transporting via truck routes, and claim the extra commission."

"That's illegal?"

"Forgery? Commission scamming?"

"Oh."

"Anyway, what my dad claims he didn't know was that when he'd drive the box trucks back to town, they were filled with pilfered merchandise. There was a gang in Vermont that was embezzling stolen items from a gang in Maine, and the whole thing blew up, so we had to leave town."

"That's insane!" Lyndsey breathed. "So, you're like, on the lamb!"

"You have a lamb?" Kate asked.

"You're a moron, Kate," Lyndsey stated, and Eliana laughed. "On the lamb, like on the run. Does the mob have a hit out on you?"

"More like an MC," Eliana said, still laughing. "I don't know if they're after me and my dad or not, but it was made pretty clear that we weren't allowed back in town. They pretty much run the whole county, so in exile we remain."

"And you haven't heard anything from Kye? You never kept in touch?"

"I tried for a while," Eliana confessed and felt her throat starting to constrict with emotion. "I'd text or call, but he never kept the same phone number for long, so I don't know if he ever got any of my messages. I wrote him a letter once, but the only address I had was to his old foster home, so I doubt he's even read it. I don't know… I guess it just wasn't meant to be. Two ships in the night…"

"First loves are a bitch," Kate concluded and wrapped a tan arm around her friend's shoulder as Lyndsey poured more drinks.

"It's fine. I'm over it," Eliana lied and dutifully downed her beverage.

"Of course you are!" Lyndsey agreed. "Look at you! Class valedictorian, head sorority sister of Kappa Delta Epsilon, second cutest girl at this party!"

"Second?"

"After me, of course," Lyndsey boasted with a sure smile.

"What about me?" Kate snapped.

"You make top ten at least," Lyndsey said callously.

"Whore," Kate muttered, and Eliana snorted in laughter.

"The point is!" Lyndsey said loudly to interrupt Kate's temper tantrum. "Eliana, you're amazing, and your friends love you. You don't need this Kye asshole to have an incredible life. You seem to already be on top of the world."

"You're right," Eliana said, but she couldn't help the feeling of longing that still drew her to the boy who danced with her every night in her dreams.

"What you need is a solid rebound," Kate suggested. "Nothing serious, just a good old-fashioned fuck fest!"

"It's been four years, I think we're past the rebound phase," Eliana replied. Regardless, Kate jumped up from the bed and retrieved her softball bat from the corner and provocatively placed it between her legs.

"We'll get you a fat donkey schlong!" she yelled, wiggling the bat and raising her eyebrows with less than subtle perversion, and Lyndsey howled in laughter.

"Donkey schlong!" she yelled in chorus with Kate, and the two began chanting the phrase. Eliana turned seven shades of red and fled the room as the two girls chased her still crying "Donkey schlong" to the amusement of everyone at the party.

* * *

ANYONE WHO HADN'T STUMBLED home or passed out on a random piece of furniture was tucked into the living room binge-watching old movies. Eliana, who had drunk way more than intended, excused herself from the dwindling party and made her way back up to her room. Kate and Lyndsey had eventually relented in their effort to 'donkey schlong' her into having rebound sex with any guy at the party, and Eliana was grateful.

The room was dark and empty when she entered which suited her just fine even though she tripped into two boxes as she did. Collapsing on her bed, she shed the jeans she wore over her swimsuit and pulled on a set of warm sweatpants and a t-shirt that proudly displayed the Harvard logo. Lying in bed under the covers, she saw the photograph still sitting on her nightstand. Slowly picking it up, Eliana felt transfixed by the memory.

Like a restless ghost, the memory of that night couldn't be ignored. As hard as she tried to think only of the good moments, the image of Kye's stoic face when her dad had literally torn her from his arms still haunted her. He hadn't even reached for her. Hadn't once said her name. He hadn't come after her.

Squeezing her eyes shut, a fresh round of tears leaked from the corners. Hadn't she wasted enough time over the last years crying over him? Sighing in frustration, Eliana rolled onto her back and dug her cell phone out of her discarded pants pocket. Scrolling through the old contacts, she pulled up the last number she'd ever had for Kye and dialed it.

It went straight to voicemail.

"Kye?" she asked after the beep. "I doubt you'll ever get this, but fuck it. My friends are right. I don't need you. You always said you were riding with the Demons for us, for me, for our future. But you know what? You're a liar. You didn't do it for anyone but yourself. If you hadn't been caught up in all that bullshit, we could have had a life together. Maybe it took four years and a college degree to figure it out, but I. Don't. Need. You." Her emphasis was pointed on each word. "That's right. I have a college degree! I graduate on Sunday, and I did it all on my own. Law school, here I come!" Her head was swimming, so she draped an arm over her forehead. "I'm going to go on to be a big, successful lawyer, probably start my own practice in New York, and one day you won't even be a memory anymore. Goodbye, Kye Driscoll. I hope you're happy with your stupid motor-cycle club, an-and your guns, and your drugs, and your criminal record, and-and your stupid donkey schlong!"

Eliana forcefully hit the 'end' button thinking it somehow equated to slamming the phone on him. She tossed her cell onto the floor and rolled over before falling into a restless, drunken slumber.

16

"Don't forget these," Kye said, tossing the black thong at the woman who was lacing up her knee-high boots. She smiled and crawled up the bed where he was reclining bare-chested against the headboard. Giving him a firm kiss on the mouth, she stuffed her underwear into the pocket of his jeans.

"Keep 'em," she offered. "It'll give me a reason to come back later."

"Like you need one," Kye said suggestively as he slid his hand between her legs. She giggled and pushed his hand away before standing. She gave him a wink at the door before she closed it behind her. Kye stretched his arms behind his head, allowing his eyes to close in bliss as he still felt the waves of his pleasure fading.

He'd set up quite the suite in the clubhouse since he'd first moved in over ten years ago. Rather than a bare cot in a room that looked like a cell, he'd been upgraded to one of the master rooms reserved especially for the officers.

Since the days of the Defectors, they'd restructured their club more like a monarchy than a business. It had been months of warfare to squash the uprising of the Vermont chapter and those who had sided with Wayne and Dean from Maine. Those who had remained loyal were sworn in to the new crew while those who hadn't… well, let's just say the worms didn't go hungry that year.

Before the sun rose each day, Kye was making thousands of dollars on sustainable operations.

The Screaming Demons now owned all of Pine Hill. They'd invested their dealings in every business in town and were now the sole import and exporters in town. Nothing came in they didn't buy, and nothing went out they didn't sell. Max had a plan to purchase the land from the state in the next few years so they could expand their compounds without pesky licensing agents running inspections.

The Demons had their kingdom and Max, the devil himself, had risen above any petty rebellion. He'd done it with Kye at his side. Kye's unwavering loyalty had more than earned him a seat at the big kid's table. It was widely known, if Pine Hill was Hell and Max was the devil, then Kye was the prince who was promised. Perfectly groomed and flawlessly executed, Kye was everything Max had hoped to find in a successor. He just had to keep playing his cards right, use his tactical mind, a little muscle when it was called for, and soon the entire organization would be his. He would have everything.

Almost.

A chirping noise from the top drawer of his dresser startled Kye out of his revelry. Padding across the white carpeted floor in his bare feet, he yanked the sock drawer open and dug around until he found the box of his old burner phones. Usually opting to swap out SIM cards, he still kept them charged in case he needed to recycle old numbers. It took him a moment to find the one that had chimed.

A flood of emotions hit him square in the chest when he saw the number and the voicemail icon in the corner. Before he could overthink it, he hit play:

"Kye?" His heart skipped a beat.

"I doubt you'll ever get this, but fuck it. My friends are right. I don't need you. You always said you were riding with the Demons for us, for me, for our future. But you know what? You're a liar. You didn't do it for anyone but yourself. If you hadn't been caught up in all that bullshit we could have had a life together. Maybe it took four years and a college degree to figure it out, but I. Don't. Need. You."

Her pointed words were like a knife to the heart.

"That's right. I have a college degree! I graduate on Sunday, and I did it all on my own. Law school, here I come! I'm going to go on to be a big, successful lawyer, probably start my own practice in New York, and one day you won't even be a memory anymore. Goodbye, Kye Driscoll. I hope you're happy with your stupid motorcycle club an-and your guns, and your drugs, and your criminal record an-and your stupid donkey schlong!"

Kye stood for a long moment, replayed the message twice, and stood for an even longer interval before he needed to sit down. She'd called him.

Eliana.

Despite the fact that the club had lost track of Henry and Eliana once they'd passed through New Hampshire, Kye knew eventually where they'd end up. No way Eliana was going to sacrifice her college career for anything. On the down-low, Kye had been able to track Henry who'd spent the last few years working on oil rigs just off the coast of the Carolinas, but Eliana... sweet, beautiful, perfect Eliana had flourished in school.

Kye dug his iPad out from under the bed and fired up the social media apps. While Eliana had done her best to stay off the grid, never creating profiles for herself, it hadn't been hard to find her on other people's pages. Especially after she joined the sorority her sophomore year.

He could always find her somewhere in the background at a bake sale, a car wash, volunteering at a soup kitchen over holidays, giving a speech to a local elementary school; he had to hand it to her— Eliana had an instinct for staying hidden. But like the sun during a solar eclipse, she was never going to stop shining.

He still had the newspaper clippings that featured her as volunteer of the year, her humanitarian award, the year she was featured in the school paper for breaking the record for most courses passed in a single semester; she was incapable of not being entirely wonderful.

Kye smiled when he saw the latest picture on Instagram from her friend Lyndsey. She and her two friends were crammed onto a single lounge chair by the pool. All smiles and perfectly tanned skin, he admired how her breasts looked in a bikini top. Wherever the shy Eliana had gone, he didn't know, but he wasn't going to complain at the feast for his eyes as he admired her body in the picture.

Then guilt set in.

His body was still tingling with the touch of another woman, and not the first he'd had since Eliana had left, yet here he was ogling the love of his life like a pinup doll. She was more than that. She would always be more than that. He was never going to be able to get her out of his head or his heart. It wasn't a new realization. Though it had been four years, he'd given up trying to forget her.

Sure, he was prone to frequent distraction. He poured himself into his work, club politics, and occasionally he buried himself between the legs of a Wall Kat, but Eliana would always be the sole owner of his heart. When Max was gone, Kye would have the power to lift the bounty on her father, and subsequently her, and then there wouldn't be anything that stood between them. That is… if she still wanted him.

Hadn't she just called?

Clearly, Eliana was still thinking about him too. Though he hadn't comprehended all of her slurred words, and he wasn't even going to begin to guess what she meant by 'donkey schlong', didn't that mean she still cared? If after all this time she was still angry, still hurt, and hell she still had his old cell phone number, then that meant she still, to some extent, carried a torch for him.

That thought brought a smile to his face. He still had

the letter she'd written him two years ago. His old foster mother, Carey, had given it to him at Stanley, her late husband's, funeral. Full of regret and a level of shame, Kye had gone to Stan's funeral after a heart attack had claimed him. He'd hugged and kissed Carey like a mother, and she'd wept on his shoulder, told him she was still proud of him, and given him the letter.

Kye had driven that whole night and into the next day to get to Cambridge, Massachusetts. In the letter, Eliana had told him how she would always love him. How even though he hadn't come for her, she would wait for him and how she prayed every night he was safe and thinking of her. When Kye had arrived in town, he'd watched from afar as she moved her boxes from her rented truck into the sorority house.

Laughing and bounding on her heels, she looked impeccably happy. How could he ruin that for her? Kye had subsequently mounted his bike, turned it around, and driven home without so much as catching her eye. He had promised himself long ago to never be the reason her life was ruined.

Though he didn't dare come for her until Max was dead and buried, he wasn't going to miss this chance to see her. Even if he remained unseen. He couldn't miss this occasion in her life.

Grabbing an overnight bag and the keys to his nicest car, he hastily packed and left the clubhouse, forgetting he still had a pair of black lacy panties in his pocket that most assuredly didn't belong to Eliana.

* * *

"PLEASE ALLOW me to introduce you to this year's class valedictorian and recipient of our first ever, All Saint's Scholarship, Eliana Granville!"

From the sea of crimson hats, Kye watched as the lone woman stood and made her way toward the front. He was positioned at the very back of the auditorium. Dressed in his perfectly tailored suit, designer shoes and with his hair flawlessly styled, he looked like one of the patrons with whom he sat. People with money were always revered.

Kye's heart began racing as he saw Eliana embrace the woman who'd introduced her, and with the dying applause, she took her place behind the podium, her smile shining as brightly as the honors cords that were draped around her neck.

"Good evening friends, family, professors, our esteemed board of directors, alumni and of course, graduates," she began in a commanding voice. "Today we welcome all because today we're marking a monumental occasion. No, I don't mean graduation," she continued with a small smile of mischief. "As those who have gone before us can attest, graduating from Harvard

University is no small feat, but it is achievable. What I'm referencing is that today is the day we graduates declare a new legacy. Today we dare to defy."

"As the recipient of Harvard's newest honor, the All Saint's Scholarship, I can tell you that a life of defiance is not a bad thing. We face more challenges than we do solutions, more struggles than ease, and more battles than victory. No, I'm not just referencing Dean Waterford's mid-terms…" the crowd chuckled at her small joke. "We are a generation of individuals who've been told 'no' at almost every turn. But not today."

"Today we stand together, staring 'no' in the face and saying 'yes'. Yes, we will struggle. Yes, we will strive. Yes, we are going to claw and crawl and bleed for our dreams because we are going to defy the odds. You can stack statistics, percentages, and odds against us, but that won't stop us. We are the class that will set a new precedent. We are the one percent, the odd-man-out, the black sheep, the underdog. Today we defy, and tomorrow we celebrate a victory. To my classmates and all in attendance: I believe in you. We are going to change the world."

Eliana looked near tears as she received a standing ovation for her emotional and inspiring speech. Kye couldn't take his eyes off her as she was handed the plaque of recognition. Even though she had no idea he was there, he felt she was speaking directly to him.

Defiance in the face of adversity.

Standing to leave the auditorium just after her name was called to receive her diploma, Kye felt more resolute than ever. It didn't matter how long it took. He would conquer the Demons and turn his kingdom into the catalyst that would secure his future with Eliana.

They would defy the odds.

17

"I'm sorry Miss Granville," Doctor Newton said, placing a comforting hand on Eliana's shoulder as she sat on the edge of her father's hospital bed. Eliana nodded solemnly, and the doctor left the room to give her a moment of silence. Looking down at her father who was more machine than man now, her chest heaved, and she felt she may vomit.

"Damnit, Dad," she cursed and stood on trembling legs. Having just heard the prognosis, she now knew that her father would never wake. His health had been declining for the last two years. First diagnosed with a fatty liver, then diabetes, she hadn't guessed it would eventually turn to lung cancer. At this point, he needed more transplants than he had organs. Two less than successful surgeries, he wasn't even on the list for a new kidney let alone able to survive the operation.

Eliana paced to the window and looked out from the high vantage point. Below her, the city of Boston continued as usual. Why shouldn't it, though? Her dad wasn't anyone important. He'd mooched off unemployment and disability for nearly three years after breaking his back while off the coast. Never mind he'd been drunk and slipped down the stairs of the rig.

The last year of his life had been in Eliana's guest room hooked up to every kind of monitor. She'd been signing over every bit of his social security just to keep the full-time nurse on staff so she could keep working. Henry hadn't been shy about complaining either. Having his left foot amputated from diabetes, he'd been bedridden for ten of the last twelve months.

Eliana felt a hot tear leak from her eye as she covered her face with both hands. Her shoulders were shaking with restrained sobs. She felt overwhelmed with guilt.

"It's not like I didn't try!" she yelled as she rounded to confront her unconscious father. "I sent you to three rehabs, didn't I? I gave you a place to live when you were going to be homeless! I hired nurses to care for you around the clock. I sat up with you, cleaned up your shit and vomit, and read to you when you lost your vision from liver failure! Didn't I try!" Her voice was shrill and piercing, but her father remained unmoving in the bed. "I tried! I tried so hard," she sobbed and sank to her knees on the floor.

The salty drops fell onto the cold tile, and Eliana felt that the whole building could collapse around her, but she wouldn't care at all. Though she'd never admitted it, she had always held out hope she could save her father from his alcoholism. There had been a stretch of nearly a year when he'd been sober, and they had been blissful.

She'd convinced him to travel with her, and they'd spent two weeks visiting the historical attractions in New England. They were memories she would try her best to cherish, but at the moment, they just made her angry. "You could have stayed sober," she said through gritted teeth. "You could have tried harder. You could have asked for help, but you didn't want it! You didn't want me—you just wanted to drink! I hate you!" Fresh tears sprang from her eyes, and she sat with her back to the wall and cried for a long time.

When she finally was able to stand, she wiped her face and composed herself. Opening the door to his private hospital room, she saw Doctor Newton and two nurses waiting for her.

"Turn the machine off," she instructed quietly, and the doctor nodded wordlessly. He moved past her into the room and with a flick of a few buttons, the apparatus that kept poor, broken Henry Granville breathing stopped pumping air. Doctor Newton removed the mask and the tube from his throat.

With a small gurgling noise and a flutter of his

eyelids, Henry Granville took his last breath. Doctor Newton gave Eliana's hand a small squeeze as he once again left the room. Eliana stared at her father's lifeless body for a moment before she took a deep breath and let it out in what she would later realize was a heavy sigh of relief.

It was over.

THE PLANE HAD BARELY TOUCHED down when Kye felt his phone vibrate. He was descending the staircase to the private plane with his duffle bag over his shoulder when he flipped the phone open and read the text.

'My office' was all it read, and Kye knew exactly what was expected.

"Have a pleasant trip?" Grier asked sarcastically as he opened the door of the Town Car for Kye.

"Successful is a better word," Kye said and handed Grier his bag before sliding inside. The beige leather upholstery was kept immaculate, and Kye loosened his tie before removing it and tossing it on to the seat next to him. Grier took his spot at the wheel, and the car was off.

Their overseas operations were booming, and Kye was now traveling every other month under the guise of an international gemstone dealer. While suits, business meetings, and corporate hedge funds weren't exactly his speed, he couldn't deny the benefits.

He'd spent the last six years building the perfect empire. He now oversaw the command of six private planes, five compounds in New England, and countless employees and personal staff. Leaving the majority of his ethical business dealings to the Brilliant Defiance board of directors, he was free to handle the shipping of contraband from the UK to the States and vice versa.

In the last years, Max had been forced to take a less hands-on approach to the club due to his dwindling health. This left room for a near takeover on Kye's part. He was close. Very close. However, these next few months would be delicate.

With the growth of the club to just under twelve chapters, a complete transition of power would need to come with a Vote of Confidence. If Kye didn't receive Max's blessing to take over completely, any number of the inner circle could cry foul, and they'd once again be faced with a rebellion the likes of which would split the empire, and it would likely crumble completely.

Max had made sure of this. Learning from his past mistakes, he insisted on inserting himself into every aspect of the club. If he didn't personally approve it, it didn't happen. While it was a good strategy for making himself indispensable, it was taking its toll. In the last few years, Max had suffered two minor heart attacks and though it was kept under wraps, rumors were beginning to circulate that he was on his death bed. That's why Kye had been called back early from his trip.

The rumors weren't far from the truth as Kye plainly saw when he entered Max's office only forty-five minutes after he'd landed. Max was seated in his usual throne-like chair but was hooked up to an oxygen tank. The Wall Kat at his side was helping him sip water through a straw, and she smiled softly at Kye when he entered.

"Max," Kye greeted and shook his hand. Max's once-powerful hands were in a permanent state of trembling.

"Get out," Max barked, and the blonde hurried out of the room. "Sit," Max ordered, and Kye slowly slid into his appointed chair directly across from him. Only the two of them occupied the office. "How was your flight?" Max asked in a hoarse voice.

"It was fine," Kye answered. "Do you really care?"

"No," Max replied and pulled the tube out of his nose.

"Didn't think so," Kye said chuckling. "We're looking good in Wexford County. I know that's what you were hoping to hear. We cleared out some of the competition, but it's probably going to get ugly before it gets better."

"You'll handle it," Max said shortly. Kye eyed him suspiciously as he stood and poured two glasses of brandy. "We've got other business to deal with," he said, passing one of the glasses to Kye.

"I had a feeling," Kye stated, taking a polite swig of the gold liquid that burned his throat. Max opened the top drawer of his desk and pulled out a cream-colored folder that he slid across the table. Kye set his glass down and flipped the front cover open.

The first image was a dual mug shot with the name Duncan Crane underneath with a rap-sheet that took up two more pages. A similar report was next with Duncan's brother, Leroy. Kye skimmed the details and let out a quick breath.

"Least of these being robberies, but murder? There isn't much hope for them, Max. We can make them comfortable, pull some connections in prison to make their last few months cushy, but they'll fry for this." Max was silent, fingertips pressed together and held against his mouth. He then opened the drawer again and pulled out a second folder. Kye set the first one aside and took the next, expecting to see more mugshots.

He froze when, instead of a stoic, ugly criminal looking back at him, he saw Eliana's college yearbook photo starting back at him. Behind it was an article from the local paper that boasted of Eliana being the youngest lawyer signed to Nelson, Watford, and Shier. There was a photograph of her house. Cell phone number. Bank information. License plate number.

On the opposite side was a similar report on Henry. However, scrawled recently in red marker across Henry's photograph was the word 'DECEASED'. Pulling the picture out, Kye saw the obituary behind it. He pretended to read a moment longer in order to gather his thoughts before looking back at Max.

"So you found Henry Granville?" Kye asked and hoped his voice didn't sound as shaky as it felt.

"I never lost him," Max stated as he leaned back in his chair and watched Kye very closely. "Looks like the old bastard bit the dust before we could collect his debt."

"It's been ten years, Max…"

"I never forget a debt," Max interrupted.

"I just mean, if you knew where he was this whole time, why did you wait?"

"You still have a lot to learn, kid," Max stated and coughed several times before he was able to compose himself. "Some things are all about timing. It's not just about collecting the debt, but when to collect it."

"He's dead, Max. Unless you're on his life insurance policy, I don't see you collecting the money he owes you."

"I'm sure you're right on that," Max said thoughtfully as he struggled to open an orange prescription bottle. Kye mercifully took it from him and popped the lid for him. Max poured a few into his hand and downed them while polishing off his drink. "You know, I always saw myself going out in a blaze of glory, not crumpled over a bottle of pills and brandy like some dementia-ridden vegetable."

"You're hardly a vegetable, Max," Kye said.

"But as fate would have it," Max continued as though he hadn't been interrupted, "I never had sons. You'd have thought with all the women I've had, at least one of those whores would have tried to manipulate me with a kid I could pass this empire to. I'm old, I feel like I've got a car parked on my chest every time I breathe. I sneeze and I piss myself. The last doctor I saw recommended I move somewhere with more sun and quit eating meat. Useless fucker."

"Want me to make you a salad?"

"Sure, go grab me a sack of those novelty carrots and shove one right up your ass," Max stated, and they both laughed which resulted in Max having another coughing fit. Kye poured him another drink, which he promptly drank. "It's no secret, all of this," Max said and gestured to the room around him, "is going to pass to you one day." Kye felt a glimmer of hope. "You're about as close to family as any bastard son I could have sired. You see," Max said as he lit a cigarette, "that's family." Kye felt realization begin to set in. "Things pass from father to son. In some cases," Max said, tapping a finger on the file that still lay open in front of Kye, "father to daughter."

"You want to milk Eli for fifty grand?" Kye asked before he could stop himself.

"Eli, is it?" Max questioned, but his tone indicated he had more answers than questions. Kye clamped his mouth shut. "I know she used to be your girl," Max said, blowing out a puff of smoke. "You still got a hard-on for her?"

"Haven't seen her in years, Max."

"That wasn't the question, boy," Max stated in his low tone that indicated he was very serious. "Your girlfriend got herself a job as a hotshot attorney. I knew if we sat back and watched her long enough she'd prove valuable. To our advantage, she deals in defense cases. We're going to convince her to take on a few of our more delicate clients."

"Her dad just died, and you want to hire her?"

"Who said anything about hiring her? She's got a debt that needs to be settled. I'll be gracious and let her work it off. Just be glad I'm letting her do it in the courtroom and not on the Wall." Max was baiting him to see just how he'd react to the idea of whoring her out. Well, Max wasn't the only one with a game face. Kye remained stoic, so Max continued. "Her dad pilfered nearly fifty grand in goods that should equate to enough time for her to get a few of our boys out of prison."

"I can assume we're not giving her an option," Kye concluded. He felt hopelessness creep in, but what was worse, Max didn't just have dirt on Eliana— he had dirt on Kye. If Max knew this much about Eliana, he likely knew everything. How Kye had made several trips to Cambridge to snoop on her. How he'd made the anonymous donation to Harvard for the All Saint's scholarship to ensure Eliana could finish law school undeterred. It was enough to ruin both of them.

"You're wrong on both counts," Max said as he finished his cigarette and dropped the smoldering bud into his empty glass. "She's got an option. Do it or die, simple as that. I don't like to leave loose ends. If your leggy girlfriend won't cooperate, then she's lost her usefulness."

"You said 'both counts'?" Kye questioned as he balled his hands into fists under the table. Just the thought of anyone touching Eliana made his blood boil.

"I did," Max agreed. "We aren't going to do anything," Max said, leaning forward toward Kye, his heavy eyebrows raising. "Iron your black suit and get to that funeral. You're going to be reunited with sweet, innocent Eli."

THAT WAS how Kye found himself pinning Eliana up against a tree outside the small, white church. Playing the bounty hunter once again, he was now sent on the ultimate errand: to bring in the only person in his life he'd ever loved. Whether karma was a bitch or just Max, nothing about this situation was easy.

After informing her that her life was no longer her own and Eliana's inherited debt amounted to a life of servitude, he'd watched her stunned reaction fade into a distracted resolve as the minister had beckoned her to accompany the procession to the burial site. Kye stood in the distance, allowing her the privacy of a final goodbye as the casket was lowered into the ground.

She stood like an angelic pillar among the gravestones. The hem of her black dress wafted in the breeze while overhead, the late spring warmth had turned cold and dark clouds rolled in. A storm was brewing. The distant thunder was evidencing enough of that. A crack of lightning split the sky, and the first raindrops began to pour.

ELIANA WAS past the point of emotion. The tears she'd had for her father's passing were spent, her nerves of presenting the eulogy had faded, and now as the graveyard attendants performed their final duty, Eliana felt herself slip into a blissful state of numbness. She couldn't feel anything at this moment.

One by one the onlookers who'd been invited to the

grave left. Even the minister had excused himself when the weather turned south. Yet still, Eliana remained. Anyone might have guessed she was grieving, maybe praying or trying to muster the strength to walk away, but in truth, she waited until the last remnants of dirt filled the hole of the grave, the turf was tucked into place, and the rain soaked the ground around her, because she knew the moment she turned away from poor, dead Henry Granville she was going to have to face the very much alive Kye Driscoll.

She could feel him watching her. It was a feeling she recognized from over the years. Every so often she would catch what she thought was a glimpse of him in the crowd, by her house, at graduation, on the bus… but it never turned out to be him. Still, what felt more shocking than seeing him, speaking to him, touching him after all these years was that nothing felt any different.

He'd had her up against that tree, and every molecule in her body had come to life as though she had just woken up. While her mind was trying to process his words, his threats, her body had pressed into him like a thirsty man after a drink of water. And God was she thirsty for him.

Shaking her head and chalking it up to grief, Eliana glanced in his direction briefly before she began the slow walk up the hill from the graveyard back to the church where her car was parked. Without a second look, she knew he was following her. The torrent of rain was picking up, the cold air blew, and the mud squished underfoot to the point where the heels of her shoes were getting stuck. In her frustration, Eliana pulled her shoes off entirely and finished her walk barefoot.

When she was back at the door to the church, only two cars remained in the parking lot— hers and one she didn't recognize. It was a black SUV with tinted windows that were obviously brand new as it still had plates from the dealership. Looking at the tree, she didn't see Kye's bike anymore. She could have sworn he was still behind her…

"Eli." She gasped in fright when she'd begun to turn to see if he was there only to find him directly behind her. She stumbled on the slippery step, and Kye caught her before she fell. Eliana felt the hard muscles of his arm as it wrapped around her, and without another thought, she sank into him. Arms wrapping around his neck, she pulled him into a tight hug, and he didn't hold back as he returned the embrace.

After ten years, they were finally together again. Though life and stubbornness had pulled them away, they had somehow found their way back into each other's arms. Kye was still as firm and unwavering as she remembered, and Eliana still smelled of honey and chocolate. Her hair, though shorter, was still soft and feathering, and Kye still dug his fingertips into her back the way he had so many times before.

Kye only broke the hold he had on her when he felt her shivering from the cold. Keeping his hands on her hips he looked her in the eye, with her on the step above him she was of equal height. He brushed her cheek with his hand, and she leaned into the touch. Unable to help it, he placed a soft kiss to her forehead, and the warmth of his mouth sent a fresh wave of shivers through her.

"Come here," he beckoned and took her hand to lead her into the now empty church. The room was darker than before, the light through the stained glass much dimmer now that dark clouds blocked out the sun, but the candles from Mass were still lit. Kye led her to the front of the church where he sat her in the front pew. He left her for a moment only to return with two hand towels from the bathroom and her coat that she'd hung up on the rack near the front door. "You're freezing," he noted as he draped her jacket over her shoulders before kneeling in front of her.

"I'm fine," she said calmly as he began towel drying her arms, hands, and face. When he wiped her cheek. she placed her hand over his and gently pushed it away before taking the towel from him and finishing the job herself. Clearly, her senses had returned, and she was now going to ask for answers over affection. "Are you going to kill me?" she asked in the same even tone.

"No," Kye answered as he removed his wet coat and sat on the step of the altar across from her. He wasn't looking at her, though; he'd dropped his eyes to his shoes where he used the second towel to clean the mud from them. "But there are people in town who will," he stated before she could ask a second question.

"All because my father committed crimes against the Screaming Demons. Crimes that I had nothing to do with?" she asked, the anger in her voice growing.

"Yes," Kye answered plainly. "Max knew all along where you and your father were. I don't know how, to be perfectly honest, but he's obviously had this planned for a long time. He's waited until the right time to collect a debt."

"Is he hard up for cash or something?" Eliana asked with bitterness, and Kye chuckled which only seemed to anger her more.

"On the contrary, Max is a rich man. The club clears about ten million a year tax-free," he teased.

"Then why? Why come after us now? Why me?" They were valid questions that Kye knew he couldn't answer, so he was silent for a moment. "Damnit, Kye, answer me!" Her voice reverberated off the walls and made him look up at her.

"Because that's what Max does," he began and set the muddy towel on the step next to him. "He finds pain points and exploits them to see if people will crumble.

Max knew you were studying to be a lawyer, and I guess he decided you were worth more with a law degree in your hand than cash."

"So what… he's got some outstanding parking tickets he wants me to take care of?" Her sarcasm was sexy, and the fiery look in her eyes was making it hard for him to keep his distance. Sitting on the church pew with mud-covered feet and soaking wet hair, he had a tempting idea to take her behind the pulpit and give the Virgin Mary a show.

"I'll give you all the details when we get to Pine Hill," Kye said, standing. Eliana dropped her chin, her eyes narrowing at him.

"Pine Hill? You're joking. I'm not going to Pine Hill." She spat the name of the town as though the very taste was bitter in her mouth.

"You don't have a choice," Kye informed her, and Eliana let out a short laugh as if to say, 'oh yes I do'.

"Kidnapping, is it?" she asked in a huffy and self-entitled tone. "Really, Kye, I don't need to be a lawyer to tell you what that means if you try to get me to go somewhere against my consent." Eliana stood too and reached in her jacket pocket to grab her phone. "A perk of being a very good defense lawyer, I've got every sheriff's phone number saved and on speed dial."

"Really?" Kye asked in an impressed tone. "Let me see," he beckoned. Thinking Kye was challenging her word, Eliana rolled her eyes as she unlocked her phone and pulled up the screen that showed her speed dials. Sure enough, at least a dozen cell numbers to the local, county, and state patrol were cued up. "Impressive," Kye said shortly as he grabbed the phone out of her hand.

"Hey!" she shouted and reached to grab it, but Kye had turned his back. "Give that to me!" Before she could lunge again, he'd popped the back of it off and removed the battery which he slipped into his pants pocket. Putting the cover back on, he turned back to her and handed it over.

"There you go," he said with a slightly teasing lilt.

"Kye, give me my battery," she demanded and held her hand out expectantly. She was five feet and six inches of fuming mad which he found endlessly entertaining. "Now!" she yelled with a stomp of her foot.

"Get it yourself if it's so important," he challenged. Eliana eyed him, her throat pulsing as she swallowed hard. Her eyes darted from his down to his pants where she knew he'd stored the battery.

"I'm not digging in your pocket to get my battery back," she claimed and placed her hands on her hips.

"Then you're not getting it back," Kye said plainly.

"I'm not kidding, Kye, give it to me." The volume of her voice was raised again, and she remained rooted when he stepped toward her.

"You know where it is," he said in a low tone, his

eyes darkening. Eliana swallowed hard again and shook her head. "What are you afraid you'll find if you go digging around?" His question was exactly what her mind was dwelling on. She knew exactly what she would find, and it likely wasn't the battery to her cell phone.

"I'm not going to Pine Hill with you," Eliana stated, hoping to deflect the conversation away to anything that didn't involve the contents of Kye's pants.

"If you refuse, there are men waiting at your house who will either force you or shoot you," Kye informed her. Eliana visibly paled, and she stepped backward only to sit hard on the bench of the pew once again.

"They're at m-my house?" her voice was trembling, and every instinct in Kye made him want to wrap her in his arms again and chase away anything that was making her afraid. He also knew that he was the only thing standing between her and the business end of a Demon pistol.

"They're at your house, your office, and probably outside," Kye admitted. "Max is dead serious about you coming back with me."

"Dead serious? Is that supposed to be a joke?" she questioned in a fierce tone. Her eyes were shooting daggers, and Kye sat beside her.

"I didn't mean it that way. Listen, nothing bad is going to happen to you as long as you cooperate. Max wouldn't have waited all this time if he was just going to put a bullet in your head."

"Somehow that's not comforting."

"There are some guys from the club who got into some trouble, landed behind bars. Max wants you to look at their cases and find a way to get the charges dismissed. He wants his strongest players in the game before…"

"Before what?" Eliana asked in a calmer tone as she met Kye's eyes.

"I shouldn't tell you this, but there's going to be a change of power soon, and Max wants his infrastructure strong. We can't guarantee that if we have boys behind bars who can share secrets."

"I get dragged back into this mess so Max can spring his buddies from jail? If he's so rich, why doesn't he just hire a good attorney? Or better yet, bribe a judge? If he's going to send you to threaten my life the day of my father's funeral, I doubt a little thing like paying off a judge or jury member is beneath either of you." Her words were harsh, and they stung, but mostly because Kye knew they were true.

"Unfortunately, he tried that. The cases seemed airtight, and no judge wanted to make headlines by overturning two death sentences," Kye explained.

"Death sentences?" Eliana said in shock. "So we're talking murder charges. If they've received the death sentence, they've probably exhausted all of their appeals. How the hell can I do anything about that?"

"Max says…" Kye trailed off. He really didn't want to have to repeat the words his mentor had spoken. Eliana's eyebrows raised as her wordless demand for him to continued. "Max says because you're not just fighting for their lives… you will be fighting to save yours too." Kye bit his tongue so hard he tasted blood after he'd said it. Eliana immediately took her eyes off him and focused on her folded hands in her lap.

"That's it then, isn't it?" she said after a brief silence. "The trap has been set." She stood and paced a few steps, one hand pressed to her forehead. "If I don't go with you, I'm dead," she began, and her bare feet padded on the floor, "but if I do go with you and try to defend a couple of convicted murders and can't get the charges dropped completely, I'm dead. Either way, I'm dead. Best case scenario I somehow manage to free these men and then I've contributed to the release of people who will likely murder again so someone else is dead! Am I right?"

"That's about the long and short of it," Kye agreed as he watched her. Pulling her bottom lip into her mouth, Eliana was the silent embodiment of emotion. He saw her go from realization to anger, to hopelessness, to panic, to resolution.

"I'm going to need my bag," she said, pointing to the

pew behind him. Kye turned to look where she was gesturing but saw nothing behind him. When he turned to look back at her, she had already silently sprinted toward the door to the church.

She was running.

18

*E*liana was grateful she'd already removed her shoes. She wouldn't have made it far if she'd still been in heels. She'd managed to make it out the front door of the church and down the steps before she heard Kye yelling her name. With her keys gripped tightly in her hands, she pressed the unlock button and yanked the door open.

Kye was much faster than her, however, and the moment she opened the door, he shoved it closed again. Eliana rounded on him and shoved him hard enough in the chest that he stumbled backward and landed hard in the mud. She yanked her car door open once more, but before she could climb inside, she heard the terrifying click of a gun being armed. She froze.

The rain was still falling hard, the cold drops like tiny needles, but not hard enough to obscure the sight of

Kye sitting in a mud puddle with a gun pointed at her. So this was it? She'd be dead not three days after her dad. Who would bury her? Who would give her eulogy?

"Drop the keys, Eli," he ordered, and she defiantly shook her head. His jaw clenched, and the muscles in his neck looked strained. "You're not thinking clearly. You're not in any danger if you come with me."

"Says the guy aiming the gun!" she replied and was painfully aware of how shrill her voice sounded. Kye slowly rose, mud now staining his jeans and suit jacket. Eliana backed up and was starting to enter the car when Kye suddenly shifted his aim and shot out the front tire. A scream tore through her at the loud sound, and she jumped a second time when Kye fired and also shot out the back tire. "Stop shooting!" she yelled and threw her keys at him.

"Stop running away!" Kye countered and ducked before the keys could hit him in the face.

"I'm not going with you!" He lunged for her and with no other escape route, Eliana dove into the driver's side of the car and tried to climb over the center console. A strong hand grabbed her ankle and yanked her backward. Crying in anger, Eliana kicked as hard as she could, her heel connecting with Kye's jaw. Yelling both in pain and frustration, he jerked her back even harder, and she slid out of the car and onto the ground.

"Why do you have to be so difficult!" Kye snapped as

he looked down at her. Mud had splattered all over her legs and dress. Her hair was soaked and matted over her face. She wiped the shorter locks out of her eyes, smudging her face with mud as she glared at him.

"Why are you even here?" she yelled back and struggled to stand. Instinctively, he reached to help her, but she swatted his hand away while simultaneously losing her balance and slipping again.

"Stop being stubborn," he said, taking her by the arms and hauling her to her feet. He didn't release his hold, and she started struggling. Pulling her against his chest to try to keep her still, she kicked his shin. "Goddamnit!" he hollered. His blue eyes turned fierce as the twig holding his temper in check snapped. Kicking her car door shut, he spun her around and shoved her abdomen first into the vehicle.

"What are you doing?" Eliana cried as Kye held her in place with a hand on her back. His hips were dug into her backside, and she felt him shifting around. One by one he grabbed her arms, pinning them behind her back, only to feel them secured in place with the tie he had been wearing. "Kye!" she yelled and pressed back against him, trying to make him move. He thrust his hips, causing her to slam into the car again.

"Stop moving," he muttered as he finished tying the silk tie around her wrists. When he was finished, he turned her around so her back was now against the driver's window. Both of them were still trying to murder the other with their eyes, and Eliana forced herself not to feel entirely humiliated that he'd just tied her up. She was still wiggling against the restraint when she saw his eyes soften. Lifting his hand to cup her face, he brushed the dirt and grass off her cheek. Eliana froze. "You're still so beautiful," he admitted out loud.

She'd been planning on kicking him again, but when his touch turned softer and his eyes dropped to her lips, her thoughts turned incoherent. Kye looked unearthly standing in front of her. His rain-soaked hair hung loosely in a half ponytail, and drops of water beaded on the short hairs of his kempt beard. The hand that had been on her cheek moved to the back of her head, and he pulled her up onto her toes before kissing her firmly.

His mouth was like a warm bonfire in this cold rain. Unable to move with her bound hands and shock, she was at his mercy, and Kye knew it. Using his height and size to his advantage, he pinned her more firmly against the car. Her soft chest rubbed against him, and his hands moved from her head to her shoulders and down her sides. The feel of her against him when she finally started to return the kiss was blissful. But it was short-lived.

Kye abruptly pulled away, and her dazed eyes turned confused before he dropped his shoulders to her stomach and hoisted her over his right side. "Kye

Driscoll, put me down this instant!" she shouted, and her legs kicked in protest.

"If you keep that up, I'll drop you," he informed her, and it was enough for her legs to still. "Good girl," he teased and gave her butt a hard smack. She yelped and started kicking again, but he had already opened the passenger side of the SUV he'd had dropped off during the burial. Somehow, he'd known Eliana wasn't going to come quietly, and toting her on the back of his bike was going to be much more difficult than a car.

"Ow!" Eliana snapped as he deposited her head first into the vehicle. Hitting her head on the underside of the dashboard, she wiggled and squirmed from the floor to try to get her hands out from behind her back. By the time Kye had reached the driver's side, she had managed to slide them past the back of her legs and now held them in front of her.

"Christ, Eli," Kye said in exasperation. He clicked the lock on the door before she could reach the door handle, and he began unbuckling his belt. Eliana's eyes widened as he yanked it free from the loops with one swift tug and he leaned over to her side of the car. Grabbing her adjoined wrists, he wove the belt through them, pulled her into the passenger seat, and hooked the belt to the handle just above the window. "Now," he said with his face only inches from her, "sit still and behave." His eyes flickered to her mouth again. "I don't have many more clothes to tie you up with," he said with a flirtatious grin. She growled at him and he laughed as he sat back in the driver's seat and fired up the car.

"Why do I feel like you've done this before?" she grumbled as she yanked on the leather belt to test how secure it was.

"What?" he asked, glancing at her with the smug smile on his face. "Tied a woman up?" he joked with a wink.

"No," she bit back at him, "kidnapped someone." Kye felt his smile falter, and he didn't reply as he shifted the car into drive and pulled the vehicle out of the church parking lot.

"Do I even dare ask how you knew where I lived?" Eliana questioned when Kye pulled the car into her driveway. To her dismay, she saw two other men sitting on motorcycles, one of which she recognized as Kye's, and smoking cigarettes. There'd be no chance of escape now. Both men were large, bigger than her father had been when he was healthy, and twice as fit.

"Don't ask questions you don't want the answer to," Kye said, turning the car off and exiting. He greeted both men with a handshake, uttered a few words that elicited laughter from them, and all three sets of eyes turned to her. She swallowed hard. Kye took a few drags off a smoke he was offered, clearly not in a hurry before he made his way back to her. Opening the door, he crouched so he was eye to eye with her. "Are you going to behave, or do I need to carry you again?"

"Patronizing me isn't going to help," she said, narrowing her eyes. Kye grinned and placed a hand on her bare knee.

"You have no idea how much I've missed you," he said with a jovial sincerity that seemed inappropriate considering she was currently tied up. "Listen, neither of us is in a comfortable situation here…"

"Really?" she interrupted and tugged at the restraints for good measure. Kye began untying the belt from the handle.

"But you need to know, if you don't come quietly, it isn't me who's going to be hauling you around; it's Bruce and Frank," he said, gesturing to the two thugs who were watching them. "Normally I'd be happy to play cat and mouse with you, but this is slightly more serious. My advice? Get cleaned up, pack a bag, and come back to Pine Hill with me. Listen to Max's proposal, do what he asks, and clear your debt…"

"My father's debt."

"It's yours now whether you like it or not."

"Well I don't like it," she snapped and yanked her hands away once they were free. Rubbing her wrists, she swung her legs out of the car and stood. Kye was forced backward. "I don't like any of this. We might have been old friends, but we're not friends now. Don't touch me again." Her words had a bite to them but also resignation. She knew she'd been defeated. Her logical mind had finally wrapped around the reality that her hand had been forced. She was trapped.

"Let her through, boys," Kye ordered when Eliana sulked down the driveway toward her house. The two men who had formed a brick wall parted, and she pushed her way through. Eliana retrieved the spare key from under a potted plant and unlocked her front door. She briefly thought about fleeing out the back, but when she heard Kye closing the door behind them she pushed the thought away. "You've got twenty minutes."

"I'm going to shower," she said, moving toward the bathroom and pausing in the doorway. "That's not an invitation," she snapped and slammed the door in his face. He chuckled when he heard the lock click. Pulling his suit jacket off, he made his way to the kitchen and rummaged through a few cabinets before finding the fixings for a fresh pot of coffee.

MUDDY CLOTHES ON THE FLOOR, Eliana slipped under the stream of hot water and began washing the mud from her body. She hadn't realized how scraped up she had gotten in the scuffle until the water stung at her scrapes. Both knees and elbows had taken a hit from the gravel of the parking lot, and her hands were sporting fresh scratches as well. The water that pooled around her feet slowly turned from murky brown to clear as she finished washing.

Turning the water off, she wrapped herself in a fluffy towel and brushed her hair. It'd been two years since she'd chopped her waist-length hair to just above her shoulders. After graduating, she'd found it difficult to be taken seriously when she'd maintained her youthful tresses. Without much thought to sentiment, she'd splurged for a trip to the salon, hacked off eight inches of hair and gotten her toes polished.

Much like that day, Eliana was forced to put on her big-girl panties and accept reality. Their past had finally caught up to them. Or rather… it had never left. How long had Kye known where she was? Staring at her own reflection after drying her hair and reapplying her makeup, Eliana had to swallow the truth: Kye had known where she was all along and had chosen not to come for her. For years she'd held out the fantasy that one day they'd be reunited and things would all work out. Well, no more. Like her long-discarded hair, she cut away the childish delusion. Kye was a Demon and had no interest in her except what he felt she owed him.

"Still…" she said softly to herself as she touched her fingertips to her mouth. He certainly had kissed her as though he'd missed her. "Probably just a ploy," she muttered angrily and grabbed her cosmetics bag before stepping out of the bathroom. She could hear Kye shuffling around in the kitchen, so she quickly padded to her bedroom.

She simultaneously packed while she was dressing, first opting for underwear then moving to her closet to grab a few outfits. Unsure of how long her captivity would last, she opted for a variety of clothes. She had just buttoned her jeans when the bedroom door slammed open, and Kye burst in.

"The fuck!" she cursed as the commotion startled her. Kye visibly sighed in relief when he saw her standing at her closet door.

"I thought you took off," he stated and moved farther into her teal and white decorated room.

"With your bulldogs standing guard? No thanks," she grumbled, and when his eyes began roaming over her, she became aware that she was still standing in nothing but jeans and a yellow lace bra. "Do you mind?" she asked vehemently.

"Not at all," he said, leaning against her vanity mirror and crossing his arms as he watched her. Clearly, he was ignoring the hint that she wanted him to give her privacy. Deciding to turn the tables on him, she took the white t-shirt she was holding and tossed it on to the open suitcase on her bed.

"Is this what you want?" she questioned in a seductive voice, her hips swaying as she walked toward him. Kye stood a little straighter. "To ride back into my life and pick up where we left off?" she continued, now standing in front of him. She trailed a finger along his forearm and looked up at him through her lashes. "Where was that again?" She held him by the back of the neck and leaned against him as she stood on her tiptoes. Letting her lips hover over his, barely brushing them, his hands dropped to her hips. "Well, that's … just … too bad!" Just as he was leaning forward, she pushed him by the chest and pulled away from him.

"What the hell?" Kye asked as she was already crossing back to the other side of the room and yanking a green blouse from a hanger.

"Let's make one thing clear, Kye Driscoll," she said pointedly as she pulled the satin top over her head and turned to face him. "I don't play the jilted lover for anyone. Whatever happened between us when we were kids is over." She sat on the edge of the bed and pulled on a pair of white Converse. "Once this nightmare is over, I never want to see you or anyone from your stupid motorcycle club again." Zipping her suitcase shut, she held it by the handle and turned her eyes back to Kye who looked baffled. "Let's get this over with."

They'd been on the road for several hours. At one point, Eliana felt herself drifting off to sleep, the gentle hum of the tires on smooth pavement lulling her into slumber. She'd dreamt awful things. Guns and drugs and someone pounding from the inside of a casket. Images of her father's lifeless body haunted her. She could still hear the final beeps of the heart monitor that had tracked the last seconds of his life. The rapid beeping was mixed with the sounds of her father gasping for air. Choking. Gagging. Clawing at his own throat.

"Hey." Eliana gasped when she felt the hand on her arm. Startled and slightly disoriented, it took her a moment to remember where she was. Sitting in the passenger seat of the SUV, fortunately, this time she wasn't tied to anything. Kye was looking at her in concern. "You were having a nightmare," he said gently. With one hand on the wheel, his other had taken her left hand. When he squeezed it, she jerked her hand away, silently fuming that the contact had made her skin tingle.

"I was dreaming that I was kidnapped from my father's funeral, shot at, and dragged back to the hell hole I grew up in… Oh, wait, no, that's not a nightmare. That's real."

"When did you get to be so sarcastic?" Kye asked, putting his hand back on the wheel. He was about full of the bitter attitude she was giving him.

"When did you become a kidnapping thug?" Eliana countered. She was sulky for many reasons, the least of them being she was exhausted and sore.

"Well, I took a few classes in college and made a hobby out of it."

"Is that supposed to be funny?" she asked, looking over at him. Kye's smile indicated he thought himself incredibly funny. "You're a criminal, Kye. This is so much worse than all the crap you used to do in high school. We're talking kidnapping, crossing state lines which makes it a felony charge, extortion, blackmail, assault, vandalism, firing a weapon within proximity of a gun-free zone, one that I'm assuming is not licensed to you which makes it possession of an illegal weapon, threatening harm with said deadly weapon…"

"God you're sexy when you act smart," he interrupted and pushed the gas pedal a little harder so the engine revved.

"Speeding," Eliana continued with insolence. Kye laughed, rich and full, filling the vehicle with a much-needed break in tension. Even Eliana had to admit that it was slightly amusing. She crossed her arms, however, as a show that she was not going to give in to him in the least.

With a heavy sigh, Eliana propped her elbow against the window and leaned her head on her hand. The car fell silent again, but this time, Eliana felt anything but sleepy. Her mind was racing. Just when everything seemed to be going well in her life, everything had to fall apart. Leave it to her father to not only die but to leave her with substantial hospital bills and now a debt to the motorcycle gang that had wanted both of them dead for the last ten years. How was she ever going to get out of this? Even in death, she was still paying for her father's mistake.

"Just couldn't help yourself, could you?" she muttered and sighed again.

"Huh?" Kye asked, glancing over at her. Eliana was about to explain that she was silently cursing her father and not talking to him when Kye spoke up. "I mean, probably wasn't the best time to kiss you," he said, referring to earlier, "but you were pressed up against me, and God it was so good to see you…"

"Okay, not what I was talking about!" Eliana said, holding a hand up to halt him. "And the only reason I was pressed against you was because you slammed me into my car!"

"You were running away."

"You were kidnapping me!"

"It wouldn't have been kidnapping if you had just cooperated," Kye defended, both of their volumes rising again.

"Don't argue semantics with a lawyer, Kye, you aren't going to win," Eliana said, effectively shutting him up. "Since you brought it up, why did you kiss me? Some sort of sick plot to exploit my former feelings for you? Because that's a low blow even for someone like you."

"Someone like me?" Kye asked defensively. "What's that supposed to mean?"

"You know."

"A criminal, right, you haven't been shy about calling me that," Kye said bitterly. "Am I really so different from what you remember?" At his question, Eliana turned to look at him although his eyes were fixed on the road.

He likely wasn't any taller, although his height seemed more intrusive than she remembered. Where he had been lean in his youth, he'd filled out immensely in the last ten years. Without his suit jacket on, his arms were exposed in his white shirt that he'd rolled up to the elbow. Gripping the wheel tightly, she could see the bulge of muscle in his arms, and she'd felt first-hand how firm his chest was. His jaw was set and had matured. The beard was a new addition, and she couldn't deny how it contributed to how attractive he was. His hair was shorter and though it was still disheveled, she could tell it was soft and thick. Kye's usually average complexion looked more sun-kissed than she remembered, and she noted a sweeping, crescent-shaped pink scar under his right eye.

He was entirely beautiful and terrifying at the same time. He was imposing and carried himself with the confidence of a man who had held his own in more than one battle. He'd gone from crisp and sharp looking in his suit jacket and name-brand button-down shirt, to roguish and powerful in his dirty jeans and rumpled shirt. With a particular sense of pride, she saw a forming bruise on his jaw where she'd kicked him.

"How did you get this?" she asked quietly as she gently touched the scar. She needed to keep her mind away from the memory of how he'd had her up against the car. Kye flinched for a moment as though she'd shocked him when her fingers touched him, but when she went to recoil her hand, he once again took hold of it and held on.

"Took a hard hit with a pair of brass knuckles a few

years ago," he explained. "Thought my eye had popped out." He was trying to make light, but her cringe made him second guess his joke. "It wasn't too serious. Just a scar now."

"That's awful," she replied. At the sound of compassion in her voice, he looked over at her. "Why would you want to be part of a world like this?"

"I told you, don't ask questions you don't want answers to."

"I do want answers. I think I deserve them," she countered. "I lost everything that night, Kye. It started out as the best night of my life. Things were finally working out with school and moving and with you... What happened after my dad dragged me away? Why didn't you come after me? Did I mean so little?"

"No!" he said abruptly. "Eli, you meant everything to me. That's why you had to go. The guys that were hunting you and your dad down, found you because they followed me. After you left, I took your dad's truck. They chased me, and I was able to get back to town before they shot the tires out. Everything got a little chaotic... there was a lot of gunfire. Especially after the Screaming Demons showed up. Patty's caught fire in the process. Sheriff declared martial law for two weeks, but eventually, we took care of them."

"Took care of? You mean you killed them?" He looked at her again as if to ask, 'do you really want to know?'. Her response was raising her eyebrows in insistence.

"Yes, we killed all of them. Including ten of our own men who had betrayed us," Kye said truthfully. Eliana shook her head and pulled her hand away from his.

"How many did you kill?"

"If you're trying to make me feel bad about what I did, it's not going to work. I've made peace with the life I've chosen."

"So you don't have any regrets?" she asked with narrowed eyes. "You don't feel bad about the things that you've done?"

"Everyone has regrets, Eli, don't patronize me," Kye retorted. "I have a family with the Demons. I'm respected, and I've made a hell of a lot more money than I could have dreamt."

"Blood money." Eliana nearly smacked her head on the dashboard as Kye slammed the brakes of the car. "What are you doing?" she shrieked as he pulled the car onto the gravel shoulder of the two-lane road. When the car was at a complete stop, a plume of dust encircling them, Kye turned to face her completely. His eyes were on fire again.

"You're pissed, I get it," he started, "leave it to your asshole of a dad to leave you with all this shit to deal with. Believe it or not, I had no idea Max still had a contract out on you or your dad. If I had, I would have dealt with it. Kept you safe. I didn't know, and now we're both stuck in this. If I don't deliver you to Max, I lose all standing with him. If you don't report to him, they'll kill you outright. It's not pretty, but that's the facts. In the meantime, save your high and mighty bullshit for someone else. You have no idea what I've been through these last ten years without you. I've made more good decisions than bad, and I challenge anyone who says they would have made different decisions given the hand I was dealt. You wanna stay mad? Fine, stay mad, but don't you dare judge me, Eliana. I don't deserve that from you. You're not the only one who lost someone they loved that night."

"Kye…" she said softly with fresh tears in her eyes. It was only then that Kye realized in his angry tirade, he too had allowed a hot tear to pour from the corner of his eye. He wiped it away furiously with the back of his hand and glared at the road in front of him. He glanced down when he felt Eliana place her hand over his. Smiling softly, he gave it a gentle squeeze. "I'm sorry. I know you haven't had it easy either…"

"I'm sorry, Eli," Kye said after taking a deep breath. "I didn't want any of this for you. If I knew of a way out, I would have taken it. As things stand, our best bet is to hear Max out, do what he wants, and get on with life. When it's all over, you never have to see me again."

"After this is all over, I'm going to take a long vacation," she teased. "Somewhere warm and tropical where I can sip a margarita out of a coconut."

"With a little umbrella?"

"Naturally."

"I know of this quaint little place in Belize. I'll talk to the owner, see if he'll let you stay there," Kye joked as he looked over at her. She was smiling at him and his stomach flipped.

They sat staring at one another for a long, quiet moment. A sense of longing and regret surged between them. As Kye continued to stroke her hand with his thumb, the sadness turned to something else, and the air nearly crackled with electricity. His eyes were burning into her as memories of her standing in front of him in nothing but a bra circulated. God how he'd missed those breasts. Eliana shifted in her seat, feeling the need to cross her legs and keep her knees close together. Kye shifted too, but only to face her more.

Leaning over the console, he tucked a strand of her hair behind her ear and held her face. Her eyes were round and full of fear, at the imminent danger or of him, he didn't know. "I like it," he said, running his hand through her shorter locks. "You've only gotten more beautiful, you know that?"

"It's the moisturizer, you know?" she said half joking. "They say to apply it in the evening before you go to bed so that..." Her sentence was cut short when he leaned completely over the seat and kissed her. The kiss was searing, and Eliana felt every cell in her body begin to surge. God how she'd missed his lips. Her logical brain turned off like lights in a power outage, and she reacted out of pure instinct, grabbing the front of his shirt and pulling him closer.

Their kiss was a firm lock of the lips, both desperate to feel connected to the other. Unable to find any rhythm, their kiss turned frantic and messy as they struggled to anticipate the other's touch. Yet at the same time, it didn't feel wrong. When Eliana sniffled, Kye broke the kiss and pulled her into a hug, his arms wrapping around her shoulders as she buried her face in his neck.

They sat holding each other until they heard the rumble of two motorcycles approaching. Bruce and Frank had fallen behind in their journey back north but now had caught up. They pulled up behind the SUV and parked. While Bruce kept his engine running, Frank hopped off his bike and made his way to the driver's side.

Kye wiped the tears from Eliana's face and sat back before rolling the window down and greeting Frank.

"Trouble?" the man asked and glanced across the seat to Eliana. His round face was partially obscured with a gray goatee even though his head was entirely bald.

"Had to take a piss," Kye replied, and Eliana noted the

way his tone of voice changed when he was talking to Frank as opposed to her. "We're ready to get back on the road."

"Want me to call ahead? Max'll want to know when we're arriving."

"Yeah, let him know we'll be there within the hour. Make sure the house is ready too." Frank only nodded. He stared at Eliana for a long moment before forcefully spitting a wad of tobacco onto the ground beside the car. Eliana curled her lip in disgust and turned her eyes back to the road in front of them.

Kye started the car, and Frank gave the roof a quick tap of his hand and stepped back before Kye hit the gas and pulled them back onto the road. Feeling a sudden chill, Eliana rubbed her arms and pulled her bottom lip between her teeth.

Neither of them said another word the rest of the trip, but Eliana felt a very distinct shiver run through her when she read the 'Now Entering Pine Hill' sign.

"Welcome home," Kye said sarcastically.

Fuck.

DARK DESIRES

~ A billionaire dark romance series ~

Dark Desire

Dark Rules

Dark Secret

Dark Time

Dark Truth

BARRE TO BAR

~ A billionaire second chance series ~

Dancing With Lies

Dancing With Temptation

Dancing With Doubt

Dancing With Guilt

Dancing With Redemption

TWISTED INTENTION
~ A billionaire revenge romance series ~
Twisted Beauty
Twisted Love
Twisted Fate

Mafia's Obsession
~ A hot mafia romance series ~
Mafia's Dirty Secret
Mafia's Fake Bride
Mafia's Final Play

Screaming Demons
~ An MC romance series full of suspense ~
Rough Start
Rough Ride
Rough Choice
Rough Patch
Rough Return
Rough Road
Rough Trip
Rough Night
Rough Love

Standalone Contemporary Romance
Billionaire in Vegas
Billionaire Hunt

Billionaire's Game
Billionaire Retreat
Billionaire On Air
A Chance To Love
Somebody To Love
Not Mine To Love

Check out Summer's entire collection at
www.summercooper.com/books

ABOUT SUMMER COOPER

Thank you so much for reading. Without you, it wouldn't be possible for me to be a full-time author. I hope you enjoy reading my books as much as I do writing them.

Besides (obviously!) reading and writing, I also love cuddling my dogs, shouting at Alexa, being upside down (aka Yoga) and driving my family cray-cray!

Get in touch at
hello@summercooper.com
www.summercooper.com

facebook.com/summercooperauthor
instagram.com/summercooperauthor
goodreads.com/summercooper
bookbub.com/profile/summer-cooper

www.ingramcontent.com/pod-product-compliance
Lightning Source LLC
Chambersburg PA
CBHW051302210726
48287CB00002B/626